ELIZA JANE

Mother's Day

LITORIA PRESS

© Copyright 2021

ISBN 978-0-6451145-0-8 (Paperback)
ISBN 978-0-6451145-1-5 (eBook)

First Published 2021
by Litoria Press, Victoria, Australia
+61 3 59852112
litoriapress@gmail.com
www.litoriapress.com

All Rights Reserved: No part of this book may be used or reproduced by any means: graphic, electronic, or mechanical, including photocopying, recording, taping or by any information storage retrieval system, without the written permission of the publisher, except as brief quotations in critical articles and reviews specifically related to the work.

A catalogue record for this work is available from the National Library of Australia

Design and layout by Yanni Dellaportas
Cover illustration by Julia Kaylock

Printed and bound in Australia
2021: Mother's Day is Book One in the series,
'A Life Recovered'.

This is a work of fiction. All names, characters, businesses, places, events, and incidents in this book are either the product of the author's imagination or otherwise used in a fictitious manner. Any resemblance to actual persons living or dead or actual events is purely coincidental.

About the Author

Eliza Jane currently lives in Melbourne's outer suburbs with her husband and two dogs, their children and grandchildren living close by. She describes herself as a 'reformed but never recovered' alcoholic who has worked tirelessly to 'fill the void', most recently as a support worker. Eliza now devotes her spare time to supporting others in the Alcoholics' Anonymous community.

Mother's Day is Eliza's first book.

Image credit: Kelly McDonald, gardenbabiesfairyart.com

What people are saying

Eliza Jane has given a brutally honest reflection of a teenager who is thrust into motherhood. Struggling to understand the adult world, Wendy is the young and naive alcoholic, who stumbles through her parenting years treading the dark and scary road of addiction and recovery. Reading this had me laughing, crying, fearful and curious to turn another page. A struggle that's resulted in losing something very precious.

Sue Ward

I loved this book so much I read it twice. Eliza's first book is brilliant. Wendy's heartfelt and gut-wrenching letters to Charlie have given me goosebumps. I can imagine that a lot of people will resonate with the characters and this story. I cannot wait to find out if Wendy gets her wish and is reunited with Charlie.

Carl S.

A fascinating ting story that so many can relate too. A straight-from-the-heart projection of life and family relationship struggles.

Kathy George

I could well and truly identify with Wendy's story of a very interesting and turbulent life. A compelling read, I can't wait for Book Two to come out so I can find out what happens next.

David F.

This book is dedicated to all mothers, old and young, who have faced the challenges of motherhood. You are all my heroes.

ELIZA JANE

My Darling Charlie,

It feels strange to be writing a letter today, but I wanted to let you know I miss you. Today is Mother's Day – did you forget? It is the first one since you came into my life that we have not spent together. I have not heard from you at all. Just a phone call or text would have been nice. It is important for me to know you are OK.

Sitting here, I look back and wonder where the years went. I know I had to stop and take a huge breath after you finished school. No more books, no more uniforms, no more arguments about not wanting to go to school. No more private school fees! No more yelling about homework or doing the dishes. It was all worth it! I was proud of myself for not only getting you this far in life, but also because I had set the ground rules for you to become a responsible adult.

I was taught that once I turned eighteen I would be an adult, with legal, financial, and moral responsibility for myself. This is the lesson I hope I have passed on to you, Charlie. It is a hard lesson I know, but an important one, especially as I have booked my ticket to go to Europe. I am so looking forward to this trip. Of course, I wanted to wait till you had successfully finished school before going away for such a long time; now we can both follow our dreams.

I am sad that we could not be together on this day. It seems even more important, now, when it feels like my whole world is on the brink of changing. Do you feel that way too? Is that why you will not talk to me? I only want the best – for both of us.

Love always.
Mum

Chapter 1

Sometimes I do not know who I am. I have always struggled to fit in. I know that I am a daughter, sister, niece, granddaughter, wife, mother, and friend. I am also an alcoholic party girl who once dabbled in recreational drugs whilst struggling with recovery, not only from addiction but from the life I thought I should have had, the life I thought I deserved. I am a woman who has gone against society's standards, and who has done everything back to front: but who am I, after all that?

I'll start at the beginning. I am Wendy, a little girl with blonde ringlets, hazel eyes, sun-browned skin, and a light splattering of freckles on her nose. This Wendy is the eldest child in a large family, the one who plays gently with her brothers and sisters, without a care in the world.

That little girl has the whole world at her feet. Where did she go? That Wendy is just a distant memory, one compiled from stories told by others, and from old photographs stored within the glossy pages of ancient albums. Time has eroded that small innocent child and shaped her into a woman — a woman I barely recognise.

ELIZA JANE

Little Wendy has so many hopes and dreams, she knows what she wants out of life. Have I honoured those dreams of the little girl inside of me? Or, have I failed her?

I should go back further, before I was born; that is when my story really starts. My mum and dad were Pat and Sally, two young people who met one Friday evening at the local hotel. Mum was having dinner with her parents and Dad was there because, well, that was where he went every Friday with his mates.

They were both so young when they met. Mum was just fifteen, still with pigtails in her hair. She attended school with Dad's sister Laura.

At the age of eighteen Dad was already a boilermaker by trade, having done his apprenticeship at the local processing factory in Murray, his home town. Known for his good looks, he was tall and slim with thick dark wavy hair. He also had a lot of charisma, which has not faded with time.

Mum has always exuded self-confidence. A strong woman, some said she had an air of defiance about her when she caught Dad's eye just days after she had moved to Murray. As he stood at the bar drinking, he could not take his eyes off her, and particularly her well-defined breasts that were larger than those of most girls her age; making her appear older than she really was. Not wanting to create the wrong impression, I am told that he tried to hide his fascination with Mum's beauty, and her breasts, by turning off the lights while he kissed her, but he failed, in his drunken state, to see that everyone was watching as the lights blinked on and off like a beacon.

Dad was very fond of the drink, but was always popular with the ladies. He broke many hearts when he married my mother. They had not been dating very long when they realised they were going to be parents. Mum's mother was outraged. She was so young, and even worse, unmarried. Shotguns were suggested by her father, prompting her fiancé to run across town back to his mother's house exclaiming "Mum, Mum, help me! He's got a gun!"

As soon as her pregnancy was announced, Mum was told by the school she would have to leave. The marriage was organised with a minimum of fuss, Nanna insisted that it be a 'low key' event, 'hushed up' to avoid gossip, which would have actually been impossible in Murray. Due to their age, they needed a judge to grant permission for the marriage. The service was held in the local church on a frosty winter Saturday morning, followed by a small reception at my grandparents' house. Dad wore the only suit he owned, a brown pinstripe single breasted jacket with matching flared pants. Mum wore a simple long-sleeved white dress with a teardrop veil.

Should they have married? In hindsight, probably not, but that was what was expected at the time. Teen pregnancy, not to mention one that was 'out of wedlock', was frowned upon in the mid-seventies. Whether or not they made the best choices, I am incredibly grateful to them for having the strength to stand up and protect me against small town gossip and the old world thinking that surrounded them. That was the reason behind their decision to move to a new town, where they could make a fresh start as a family.

In Murray, Pat had been struggling, not only with the gossip, but his drinking problem as well. Each time he went out with his mates for just one drink, he found he could not stop, and regularly came home drunk. With their families' blessings, my parents saw moving to a new environment as the best way to build a good life for their own family.

❖

Mum and Dad bought their first and only property together in the small town of Bunji in the Victorian High Country. Dad had found a job in a local factory; they moved in and quickly established themselves in the community. Nestled in the hills, the house was so cold in the winter that Mum had to leave the hot tap dripping to prevent the pipes from freezing.

Even though I was very young for the whole time we lived there, I have a strong memory of this house. It was an older style home with a veranda that started at the front door and wrapped around the left side of the house. The house itself was oddly shaped, with the bedrooms at the front and the living areas towards the back. There was only an old wood stove in the kitchen for cooking and heating. Off the kitchen was the sunroom which I think was a later addition. The sunroom covered the length of the house; this was my playroom. The bathroom was outside, attached to the back of the house under the veranda, and the toilet was on the opposite side. I remember the tall skinny conifers that grew in the neighbour's yard alongside the driveway, providing a distinct border between the two houses.

One of my strongest memories of this time was when I was around four years old; I was sitting in the lounge room watching a show on TV, probably Play School or Sesame Street. It was an old black and white set that required a thump or two on the side when the picture became blurry, like a snowstorm was moving in across the screen. I was distracted from the show by a commotion outside; when I looked through the window, I saw men running up and down the stairs of the house next door. I climbed up on the chair closest to the window with my palm resting under my chin, watching them, I was not very happy when my mother bundled me up and took me outside just as the they were putting out the flames on the outside shed.

My parents doted on me. Mum fed me every time I cried, thinking it meant I was hungry. I was put on my first diet at the tender age of six months to reduce my chubbiness. Mum was so young and inexperienced, but she did the best she could for me. I don't know if it was to show me off, or to give Mum a small break, but my father would sometimes take me to the pub with him, where he would perch me on the table so I could see what was going on. The barmaids would bring him his pot of beer and give me a cuddle, only to discover my bottom was soaked. Together they would lay me on the beer-soaked carpet to change my nappy.

I was, and still am the apple of my father's eye. He often remarked that I was so pretty that I would be Miss Universe one day. I soaked up the attention and did not like it one bit when my sister Lynda was born a couple of years later. I hated sharing the limelight and was often mean to my new sister, refusing to share my pram and trying to tip her out of it. She was there to stay, though, despite my best efforts to get rid of her, but unfortunately, she developed breathing problems – which meant moving away from the High Country.

❖

The day of the move to Gunyah, a little town not far from Murray, I stood in the window of the sunroom watching our furniture being loaded onto a truck. I was sad to be leaving my house, which is how I thought of it, and my fondness for it has stayed with me ever since. I tried not to get attached to any new house afterwards, which turned out to be a good idea. We moved often, sometimes only spending a few months in the one place. Over the course of my childhood I attended three kindergartens, eight primary schools, and then two high schools. All the moving around made it difficult to make friends. I never wanted to become too close to other kids, knowing I would only leave them behind.

Mother's Day

When I was in grade three. I did take a risk, becoming friends with a girl from my class. I really loved spending time with her and her family; they were Russian migrants who seemed so different to us. At home, they spoke in their own language, and as I was a bright kid with a good ear, I picked up enough Russian to be able to understand their questions well enough to be able to answer in English. It made for interesting conversations.

When I discovered my family was moving again. I hid away from my friend at school, I did not think I was worthy of being the girl's friend any more. What was the point? I would never see her again. By then, I had felt the heartbreak of leaving friends behind so many times, and I thought it was easier just to turn away from the friendship. This was a big life lesson for a girl of seven: switching off my emotions to protect myself from harm became a skill I would come to use many times.

Even so, each time we moved, I hoped it would be the last one, so I could just stay at the one school and make lots of friends. Maybe I would even get a pony, like all the other girls. Friendship was something I craved constantly, and a feeling of belonging, just not within my family. I still have a couple of friends from my childhood, but not many. It was only as an adult that I have formed lasting friendships.

❖

As a child, though, I didn't want for company. In addition to my own siblings, I am lucky to have grown up in an exceptionally large family, I have always felt safe there. Dad is one of six and Mum has four siblings, so I have many aunts, uncles and cousins. Growing up in this environment provided endless fun. Holidays were spent visiting Mum's and Dad's families, and gatherings often involved both sides. I remember the card nights, Dad's mother, Gran, would sit with a shandy competing against Mum's Dad, who we called Pop. It was a fierce competition. Meanwhile, my cousins and I would be playing tiggy or some other game in the yard. On Christmas Day, the cousins were relegated to the sweltering patio while the adults crammed into the dining area to eat their meal.

Dad fitted in with Mum's parents right from the start because, like him, they were very social people. It seemed like there were always people at Nanna and Pop's place; they were hard working folk who enjoyed a beer after work on weeknights and on the weekends. Each summer they took their grandchildren camping on the river that flowed around Murray. On hot days, while Nanna was in town getting supplies, we would spend hours making fly screens out of the ring pulls from the beer cans before crushing the cans and taking them to be recycled for cash.

During the holidays, we all had our jobs to do. Nanna needed help making the jams, pickles, and chutneys, and with bottling the fruit. It was a never-ending production line. The adult women in our family would teach the girls new skills every year, while Pop taught the boys how to make fishing lures, or they helped him out in his shed. It was a privilege to grow up in a family that worked together in harmony. Although, Dad was never close to his stepfather Tony, often clashing over how things were done. Tony passed away when I was about six years old. I don't remember much about him, except being frightened whenever he popped out his glass eye to show me.

Gran was a gentle and quiet woman who walked everywhere; she never drove a car. She had a wicked sense of fun and was forever telling Dad off about his offensive sense of humour. Gran used to take us for long walks along the river, telling us about her life growing up in Murray, and about how it had changed. She would also make up stories to keep us entertained. Toasted tomato sandwiches and scones with jam and cream were always on offer, and if my uncles were not coming over we would get their share of shortbread as a treat.

❖

With each move I tried hard to make it an adventure. Mum and Dad always put a positive spin on it, so I tried to see it as something new and exciting too. However, underneath all this was the issue that my father's drinking was becoming worse; he knew something was wrong but maintained the effort to keep going every day for the sake of his young family. He was yet to have his light bulb moment.

ELIZA JANE

When my first brother Peter was born Dad hit rock bottom. A night of heavy drinking led to his defining moment – the one that eventually comes to all alcoholics – forcing him to make a choice between continuing to drink and giving up entirely. It is the hardest thing an addict will ever do, making that choice, and when you do, your life and that of those around you changes forever.

Dad finally received help through the Alcoholics Anonymous 12-Step program, and Mum went to the sister group for people living with an addict, called Al-Anon. I was five years old; I remember Dad's sponsor visiting us, we were asked to call him Uncle. He was a good man, we just thought of him as a new non-relative that we had adopted.

Dad's rehabilitation involved moving back to Murray so we could have support from both sides of the family, which was especially helpful as another brother, Nathan was born during the first year of Dad's sobriety. My parents were still so young; Dad was twenty-four and Mum just twenty-one. They had endured so many changes over the first five years of their marriage. They had bought a house, sold it, and moved several times with four children under the age of six. Now they had gone through the first toughest year of sobriety while still working hard to keep the family together. Like their parents before them, the attitude was to uphold a good image and to not air the dirty laundry, so as children, we were never subjected to our parents' struggle, they were intent on keeping us innocent and unspoiled.

Mother's Day

As an adult I began to understand why Dad preferred to stay away from other drinkers, which in my family meant missing a lot of gatherings. For any alcoholic, it is a tough gig trying to find where you fit into the world when you do not have a drink in your hand. Learning to live life on life's terms without something to fall back on to, to take the edge off, to numb the senses is hard. Raw emotions are a difficult thing to deal with at the best of times, let alone when you are around a lot of drunk people.

Once sober, we see things quite differently to those around us. We see what's true, what's real, in people, the side that people do not like showing others. It scares people when they are in a room with a sober alcoholic, they might feel intimidated and try defending their own drinking habits. For alcoholics in recovery, it is confronting to watch others in their drunken state. This makes us super sensitive about those around us and ever alert to situations that might compromise our resolve.

❖

Moving back to Murray was easy in many ways. Dad always worked long hours to support his family, holding jobs as a boilermaker, factory worker, meat process worker, apple juice plant operator, and his favourite job – the one he always goes back to – truck driving. Working was the best way to keep busy and to keep thoughts of drinking, or not drinking, from his mind. Alcoholics feel empty inside when we stop drinking, a huge cavity opens inside us that we constantly try to fill. Work is one of the things to take our minds off the fact that our lives have changed so dramatically. That is why many sober alcoholics become workaholics.

My sister and brothers and I would listen for Dad coming home from work late at night. This was often the only time we got to see him through the week. We waited to hear the television come on and then get out of bed, sneak into the lounge room and watch whatever was on with him. I loved to curl up on his lap and be wrapped in his embrace; he would kiss the top of each of our heads and we would feel safe. He would change the channel to SBS to try and get us back to bed, presuming that because it was in other languages and about other cultures, we would not like it.

I loved it all. Watching foreign shows, my imagination was set free. I was fascinated by the world outside my own neighbourhood. I already felt like a bit of a gypsy and had developed an appreciation of history, I loved reading anything I could get my hands on. Encouraged by my family to use my imagination and to not let anything or anyone stop me, it was around this time that I started to dream about travelling the world, to see for real what I had seen on TV.

❖

My mother was a mostly a housewife while she was married to Dad. We were never a two-car family; Dad always took the car to work and worked different shifts which would have made it difficult for Mum to work. Plus, having four kids to look after was enough for anyone. We always went to school with our lunches packed, and she was always there to greet us when we got off the bus.

Mum has always had a great love for reading, and she is an exceptionally good poet and a talented artist. While bringing up five children occupied most of her spare time, these skills did come in handy with our schoolwork, especially in art projects. Mum made the most amazing volcano when I was in Grade 6. I will never forget it. Instilled with the understanding that our imaginations were limitless, and that anything was possible, there was no such word as 'can't' in our household; it showed a defeatist attitude. It was not even in the dictionary back then. Nowadays, when I think of 'can't' I have to put a positive twist on it.

To help with my reading, Mum encouraged me to read the newspaper out loud. She was, and still is, a grammar queen, forever correcting us, while Dad is a typical Aussie larrikin who loved to drive my mother nuts with his improper English, but he wanted his kids to have a good education as well. Usually a big softy, he was an impatient teacher who became quickly frustrated when we could not pick things up quickly. I remember we were sitting in the kitchen one day and he was trying to teach me how to spell 'around' and 'factory'. He was two years sober at the time. Try as I might, my young brain could not grasp the words, but I did not want to disappoint him. I wanted to continue being the apple of his eye, so I really tried, but it was no good. I was worried about the consequences of not being perfect, but as it turned out, I was worried for nothing, Dad soon forgot all about it.

My parents' attention to our education helped to develop my natural storytelling instincts. Whenever we were on long trips, we would have to find a way of entertaining ourselves without fighting, which was hard when there were four of us cramped in the back seat. I often passed the time looking out of the car window at people in their front yards or walking down the street; I wrote whole stories about their lives in my head. It did not matter who they were, an exciting story would be created as their whole life flashed through my mind like a movie playing in my head. Their story went through childhood, adolescence, marriage, children, occupations, everything they had done, including the reason they were in that particular place right at that point in time. It all started with questions. That woman who was standing in her front garden watering the plants, was she lonely, hoping for someone to come past and talk to her? Was she afraid to go inside after a fight with her husband? At this stage in my life, I did not understand death, so imagining she might have been grieving the loss of a loved one, or that she might be living on her own by choice, were things that did not enter my mind.

❖

Mother's Day

Always an anxious child, I needed constant affirmation. While I know they always loved me, Mum and Dad were busy, Dad with his work and Mum looking after the house and all of us, so they were not always available to provide me with the comfort I need. I remember this especially when we were moving to a new house. This is what led me to my guardian, the willy wagtail. Or, rather, it led him to me. The first time I remember seeing one of these little birds was after we left the house in the High Country. After that, I always looked out for the willy wagtail that was there to greet me whenever we moved to a new house. I would worry if he was not there when I arrived, it would give me a sense of doom. I felt that the little bird was my only true friend, sent to protect to me. As long as my little feathered friend was there waiting for me, I felt safe and knew that everything was alright in my world.

When I got lost in depression for a few years during my adult life, I did not see a willy wagtail for an awfully long time. This increased my sadness and sense of isolation. It was not until I started healing again that I was visited by one. After that I did some research and found out this little bird is a fighter who does not take kindly to birds that boss him about - a lot like me, really. I am sure he was sent to watch over me because I needed a kindred spirit and a protector – as long as I was on the right path.

ELIZA JANE

My Darling Charlie,

Looking back, I see that your childhood and mine were similar in many ways. They were both chaotic but built on love. We both grew up in families that were always there for us. I never excluded your Dad or his family from our lives after we split because I knew how important it was for you to grow up knowing them. Even after my own parents separated and divorced, I was never denied access to both sides of my family, for which I am forever grateful.

I know we never had very much money, but I did everything I could to make our lives happy and fun filled. I did a lot of things differently to the way my parents did, but I know that I inserted the same principles into our lives. Raising one child is certainly different to the seven that made up my family, and you and I grew up in quite different eras, but I tried very hard to be the mother you wanted, while at the same time trying to remember the person I was. The lines blurred a lot more times than they should have. I realise that now.

My childhood was one of constant change: moving house, changing schools and having to give up friendships were traumatic for me. So, when it came time for you to start school, I tried to choose the right one at the start, so you would have a sense of stability – this was something I always yearned for, the feeling was strongest when I visited relatives who always lived in the same house in the same town, they never seemed to move. I did not want you to ever feel the same heartbreak of losing someone you had developed a bond with, like I did with my Russian friend. Even at that time, with the heartbreak I felt leaving behind my best friend at the tender age of

Mother's Day

eight, I decided I would never move my children's schools if I could help it.

When I think of the way I my stopped seeing my friend It makes me feel cruel and aloof, but it also taught me how to separate myself from people, to create a protective barrier. I have put up a barrier between us now Charlie, because I do not know how to bring down yours.

You and I both grew up in a sober alcoholic home, except that I made sure you were aware of it. I talked to you openly about it. I never wanted you to grow up and ask why I had not explained, why I tried to hide it from you. But then, would you have questioned it? By the time you were a toddler I had stopped drinking, you had no knowledge of my past, nor did you have to live with me as an active alcoholic.

I made the choice not to exclude anyone from your life due to alcohol, including your father. I thought it was important that you see the difference drinking makes to people's lives, so you would be in a position to make the right choice as you became older. I did not want you to become an alcoholic, I still do not want you to, I have lived with this fear most of your life, but I knew that closing down the conversation, and hiding its effects on people would not help, you had to see both sides. I wanted you to make up your own mind.

You told me once that I worked too much, was never home because of it. Work certainly filled the emptiness to an extent, but, more than that, this was the only way I knew how to give you the private school education that I thought you deserved. I find work is easy, especially when it is repetitive, and now, it takes my mind off worrying about you and missing our old life.

I was also raised as you have been, to work for what you want and to not to bludge of the government for handouts. When I first left your dad and become a single mother, I had to live off a pension to help us survive, but that money was never going to be enough for the life that I planned for us. I waited until you started Kindergarten so I did not have to pay childcare expenses, then I worked in whatever jobs I could to help us move forward. I am proud of the work that I have done through my life and the achievements that came with it. Your dad was never going to help us live the life you wanted. A life of me being at home every day for you to come home to was a fantasy that our single income household could not afford.

I am sure that all parents look back and wonder how they could have done things better. You will one day I am sure.

Love always.
Mum

Chapter 2

My childhood was chaotic, but I was loved. Thanks to the strong family unit I was a part of, I was sheltered from the harsh realities of the world until the year I turned thirteen. Then, in the space of one year, life as I had known it was gone, along with the innocence of childhood. I was caught between worlds.

On the brink of adolescence I had no sense of what was to come, but it was exciting. Starting high school, for the first time in my life I was in my element.

I was happy to say goodbye to primary school. Grade 6 began well, I started the year in a tiny school called Lavender Fields which was so old that the teacher rang a hand-held school bell to signal the start of the school day. I was voted School Captain the first week of term, mainly because I was new, and the other kids did not like the other girl who wanted the position. I was surprised and humbled by the honour.

Halfway through the year, though, my short-lived happiness came to an end when Dad was offered a better job opportunity back in Malus, which meant changing schools once again. Having attended Malus primary school for a very short time a few years before, I wasn't too worried. I was excited to see if anyone remembered me.

The first person I saw was Betsy Button, a girl I remembered. There had never been an issue with Betsy then, but things had clearly changed. As I was travelling home on the bus after my first day, I become aware of sniggering and name-calling from the back row. It was Betsy, with some of the more affluent kids joining in. This was the start of a bullying experience that I would not wish on my worst enemy, it continued the next day and escalated to the point where my siblings were too scared to play with me in the school ground for fear of losing their own friends. I was coming home from school every day in tears, begging my parents to move me to a new school. Mum and Dad both had discussions with the school on various occasions about the bullying that I was receiving, only to have it stop for a day or two before the torture began again. It was a harrowing end to my primary school years.

With the start of the new school year, I felt safe at Bloom High knowing that Betsy would be at another high school. There were now five children in our family following the birth of my brother Samuel. We were living in a house on an apple orchard. I loved living there; I have great memories of that place. We had hours of fun in the orchards playing flashlight tiggy with the bosses' children. I remember hiding up high in the giant pine trees until a mother possum came down to scare us away. We spent days walking along the creek at the bottom of the property. We picked blackberries and Mum made us more desserts than we had ever had in our lives. I remember sitting on a motorbike for the first time and falling off, getting up and dusting myself off with a laugh.

Mother's Day

I experienced my first real crush, felt his wet kisses all over my face, stolen in the night when no one was watching. All these memories have remained tucked away, safe and secure – precious moments, life would never be the same again. Comfortable in my surroundings, I had no idea that my safe haven would soon be ripped open and my life torn apart.

Two major events were soon to bring huge changes to my family, changing how we all interacted with each other, as well as with the rest of the world.

The first event was Mum finding out that our Nanna, her mother, had incurable cancer. We had not experienced death and had no idea what it really meant. Mum would travel into the city most days with baby Sam and sit by her mother's side in the hospital. Nanna was an extraordinarily strong woman, she always had something to do: knitting, sewing, embroidery, gardening, cooking, you name it. She would not allow us to visit her in hospital, so we went on with our lives as normal. We had been told that she was sick but did not realise what 'incurable' meant.

At the same time, my parents' marriage was failing quickly. This led to the second major event for the year, the most unsettling one, that saw my family being torn in two. My parents announced that they were separating. How could my parents be separating, I wondered? Until then I had never seen them have a fight or heard a bad word between them. They always looked lovey-dovey and kissed each other often. It did not make sense, and it came as such a shock because we had been protected from their fights.

It became real when I heard my mother driving off in the middle of the night. She thought it would be better for us to stay with Dad, so we did not have to change schools again.

Dad had a new woman in his life. Not new, exactly, Penny was a family friend; they had not meant to fall in love, but they did. It was too much for my mother to bear as they had been friends for many years.

It was all very confronting and confusing. Not only was I a hormonal teenager, but now Nanna was sick, and my parents did not love each other anymore, Penny was sleeping in my parents' bed and I had a stepsister Anna, so now there were six of us.

❖

Within a week, Mum came to collect us and took us back to Murray where we all stayed with my grandparents while she looked for a house to move into. It was a little crowded and I felt quite sad at how our lives had been disrupted so severely. My grandparents did everything they could to help Mum deal with her separation and impending divorce. Managing a household with five very lost and unhappy children while their own health was declining must have been difficult, but they never said a thing, not that we would have heard it anyway. We were not encouraged to speak about our grief either. My gentle grandfather once quipped while we were all talking, "Children should be seen and not heard.". This certainly made us sit up and watch our manners, even though we were generally good kids who were well-behaved and respectful.

Mum applied through the Housing Commission for a place, now that she was on her own it was all she could afford. We were lucky, living in a small town meant there was not a long list of people waiting for government housing.

The house we moved into was brand-new, just two doors up from the house we had lived in when Dad began his recovery program from alcoholism eight years earlier. I could remember when the block our house now sat on was vacant, it looked out over the orchards that surrounded the town. The orchards were still there, but now the view was obstructed by all the new houses.

I quickly reconnected with an old friend. Our families were in a similar situation, Mum and Erin's mum had been friends when they were all married. Although it was a sad situation for all of us, it was good to have a friend who understood, and it made the transition easier, especially when my grandmother passed not long afterwards.

❖

I had my first experience with the spirit world when Nanna passed. At 2.20 in the morning, I was woken by an extremely bright light in my eyes. It was not until the morning that I realised what had happened. When my aunt told me the news, I was able to tell her the exact time that Nanna had passed, it was when the light blinded me. My aunt was shocked, and a little spooked by what I told her.

As the eldest sibling in the family, I felt that the responsibility of helping my mother should have fallen on my shoulders. I helped when I could, but really, I was just a young girl trying to wear big-girl pants that did not fit me yet. Mum was the one that kept the roof over our heads, who put food on the table, and clothes on our backs. She also looked after her father and helped him to learn to cook and look after himself, as her mother had done everything for him throughout their married life. My only real job was making sure my brothers and sister were okay when my mother was not at home.

❖

As we settled into our new life, Mum reconnected with three brothers that she had known for a short time while she was married to my father. The brothers came from a town called Eureka which was one of the coldest towns I have ever visited. It was even cold in the summertime. The brothers loved coming to Murray to let their hair down, they were fun-loving boys who adopted us as their own. Dad had worked with the two older brothers. Grant and Tom, in the meat rendering factory and they had formed a close bond. Mum had nursed both Dad and Grant back to health when they became ill due to working with diseased animals.

The brothers were real bush boys. They loved nothing more than camping and fishing along the river. They taught me how to catch yabbies, we all went bush bashing, it was such fun. They went a bit too far when they took me to see a calf being born, just like real brothers they thought it was a great joke seeing me turning green.

The boys would show up regularly on Friday afternoons, ready for a weekend of fun. We could hear them roaring up onto the front lawn in their ute, yahooing and disturbing the neighbours.

I was so happy to have these young men in my life. Grant, the eldest, took the role of the father, looking after his brothers, making sure they were okay and behaving themselves, well most of the time, anyway. The middle brother Tom was, and still is, the gentle giant of the brothers. The youngest of the brothers was Beau, a real daredevil. Beau hated being told what to do, but he always listened when his brothers spoke.

One Australia Day long weekend, a music festival was held in town featuring an all-Australian line-up. This weekend sticks in my memory for many reasons, but it was also the last time I saw Grant, although I did not know this at the time. At the festival, Grant took me aside and told me that Beau was in love with me, but that I should not get together with him, it was not a good idea. He made me promise, which I did because he sounded so serious. I didn't tell anyone, including Beau, about this conversation.

When I made that promise, it was to a man I had thought would be around forever. I had no idea Grant was tidying up loose ends. Later the next week Beau rang, I was the one who answered the phone. Beau said he needed to talk to Mum, but she was out. I begged him to tell me what was wrong. I could tell he was crying. He told me that while he and his brothers were at work that day, Grant said he was going home as he did not feel well. When Tom and Beau arrived home, they found their brother in the bathtub. He had taken his own life. Tom was so mad at his brother that he punched him in the face.

On top of everything else that had happened in our lives, the pain and sorrow of Grant's death was fierce. At fifteen years of age, I felt the full force of grief. I simply could not understand why he did what he did.

Tom and Beau still visited on a regular basis, and life went on, but with a gaping hole, a hole that could never be filled, because Grant would never be with us again.

ELIZA JANE

My emotions were very raw at this point in my life. I was on the verge of my first experience with depression. Anxiety was building, it felt like it was forming a large knot in the pit of my stomach. I kept pushing it down deep inside, hoping to force it away. I was able to keep going for a while, but I did not know then that this was just a coping mechanism, not a permanent fix.

While I was still trying to deal with Grant's death, something happened that rocked our family yet again. A man Mum had briefly dated came over one night while we were all watching television; Mum had had a few drinks and halfway through the movie announced she was tired and was going to bed. I felt uneasy when the man said he was going to stay and watch the end of the movie. Once the movie had finished, he got up to put his coffee cup in the sink. My intuition had kicked in by then, I was uncomfortable having him in the house and was waiting for him to leave so I could lock the door. When he did not reappear after a few minutes I went to investigate. Guided by my inner spirit, I did something I would not normally do, and opened the door to Mum's bedroom. Peering in through the darkness, I made out a movement and quietly said, "I don't think you should be in here.". My voice woke my mother, who quickly realised what was happening to her. I was witnessing my mother being raped by a man who was supposed to be her friend. I was confused and afraid, rooted to the spot, knowing this was so wrong but not knowing what to do about it.

"Get out of here!", Mum said. I thought she meant me, so I took off out of the house and headed into town. I wandered around for a little while, and on my way back I picked some roses for Mum to say I was sorry for intruding. I arrived home grateful to see the man had gone, but worried to see Mum in a teary mess. She was happy to see me, and told me I was not in trouble, that I had saved her. We called Erin's mum and asked her to come to the house to keep an eye on my siblings, who had, thankfully, had slept through everything, while Mum and I went to the local police station to report the rape.

It was shortly after that night when the knot in my stomach burst. I could not get out of the foetal position; Mum found me curled up in a ball crying with the pain and took me to the local hospital, where the doctor informed her that I had suffered a breakdown due to the stress of everything I had been through. Depression would be something I would battle for the rest of my life.

My mother and I were referred to the local sexual assault centre in the nearby town of Stoney to get counselling. The doctors referred me to counselling as well. It was a godsend to be able to talk to someone about what had happened to my mother, about what I had seen. I was able to learn about meditation and how to calm my thoughts.

The sexual assault centre helped me to prepare for the court appearance, meaning Mum and I would need to face her rapist. I was definitely not looking forward to it; I had never been in a court room, never stood in front of a judge. I got nervous just standing up in class to give a presentation.

When I thought about being in court and talking in front of the judge and the police officer, I remembered the time when I was a little girl and our Sunday School teacher had taken us to visit to the local police station. We must have been learning about deadly sins or something; I vividly recall the police officer manhandling the teacher and throwing him into the prison cell. We were all terrified! The police officer said, "If you are naughty this is what will happen to you!". It is an image that has always stuck with me.

Since that time, I have never wanted to be trouble with the law, and even though I was clearly not in trouble, standing up in the court to tell my side of the story was terrifying. I was so nervous that I kept smiling to try to cover it up, and I felt unsteady on my feet. The officer behind me came closer when he realised I might pass out.

The court trial went on for about a week. We sat outside every day waiting for the verdict. We were extremely disappointed when the man got off for what he did to Mum. I cannot give him a name, I have erased it from my memory. Even his face is scratched out. I felt guilty that I had not done enough, maybe if had I not smiled, or had not been so nervous while in the stand, I might have helped to put him behind bars. I was angry and hurt, not only at the injustice, but because the consequences of his actions had for our family. We found out later that the man who raped Mum was a snitch for the police and a well-regarded member of the Murray Businessmen's Club. He had plenty of mates to vouch for his character, making sure he got off the charges.

The saddest part of this episode for me was that Dad, now a new father to my youngest and last brother Tom, did not believe Mum had been raped. He accused her of lying, and me of making things up. I was resentful towards my father for a long time; for the first time in my life, I did not feel I had his support. Why didn't he believe me when he knew I was a witness to what had happened? This whole situation made me resentful of older men, and of the legal system in our country. Just a few years later, while these events were still playing over and over in my mind I would be a mother myself. I did not know then how far I would go to protect myself and my child from harm, I never wanted to have either of us go through what I went through with Mum.

❖

Meanwhile, life went on. Once again, I was picking up the pieces that I thought I had carefully put back into place, whilst still trying to figure out who I was. Moving back to Murray and starting at the local high school, I already knew people from my early primary school years, and then again for six months in grade five. At least here I felt a sense of belonging.

After Mum's ordeal, school life and being with friends were great distractions, I could forget about what was happening at home. I could sit in class with my friends and hang out after school. As per our house rule, I was always home by five thirty, or at least gave Mum a call to ask if I could stay out later. Soon enough though, I was starting to bend the rules, and would laugh and make a joke when Mum became cross in an effort to get myself out of trouble. Sometimes it worked and sometimes it did not. I knew not to push Mum too far, or I would invite her scorn.

I wanted to keep my father from knowing that I was discovering boys. I could not hide it from my mother, and I did not really feel the need to, in general. But I lived in a small town, I knew everything that I did was witnessed by someone and Mum would find out, and eventually Dad would too, so it was easier to confess to whatever I had done.

As time went on, Mum became increasingly frustrated with me, our relationship soured quite a lot for a while.

I had a different boyfriend every month. In hindsight, I should have known better and waited, but it was too exciting, and I loved all the attention I was getting. It is something that I took with me into adulthood, the naïve thought that I needed someone else to love me in order to be acceptable as a person. Instead of developing skills and knowledge to become an independent, self-fulfilled woman, I was developing unhealthy co-dependence tendencies by needing to be loved instead of loving myself.

For now, I did not feel like an outsider any longer. I could go to parties and Mum would have social occasions at our house. Erin and her mother were always there. These were fun and exciting times. I felt happy, finally.

I thought I was very grown up, but I still had so much to learn, so many things to experience. I was an introvert who put on a brave face to the world and showed a side that I thought others wanted to see. There were only a few people I really trusted, and there were those I trusted more than I should have. I was still so unsure of myself; my faith was very superficial, and I was very shy. Not that anyone would have thought that, because once I had found my love – alcohol, my alter ego kicked in and I was the life of the party.

❖

Alcoholism crept up on me. At first it was just a little bit, a glass or two on the weekends, under Mum's supervision. She thought it was safer to let me drink at home than to go behind her back, get drunk and maybe hurt. But this did not immune me against problems; my drinking escalated very quickly, until by the time I was sixteen, all it took was one drink to cause me to black out every time. That didn't stop me, I loved the weekends, especially when I discovered the bad boys. Alcohol and boys do not mix very well; drinking took away my moral compass and my self-esteem really took a bashing. My memory of events that happened during blackouts is hazy, and were sometimes not triggered until years later.

Some of my friends were seeing boys who were involved in car theft and other small robberies, they smoked pot and broke all kinds of laws, becoming known as the more respectable young men to be avoided by the respectable people in the town. These were the misfits that mothers did not want their daughters to date.

I did not want to be one of those misfits who defied authority, I wanted to be a good girl who led a good life, the one my parents expected of me, but I was drawn into it. I wanted revenge for the injustices that had happened in my life, I wanted to just let fly see how far I could go. I was starting to feel suffocated by social norms. I was introduced to boys who hung out at their mate's unit up the road from where I lived, falling for the leader of the pack, Johnny, who was known to everyone as Slash.

My mother hated Slash and didn't want me to see him, but I refused to listen. In hindsight, as an adult and a mother I could see she was right, and that I was naïve and stupid.

At sixteen, I saw Slash as the perfect catch: tall, slim, with the hottest mullet I had ever seen. His stone wash jeans were ripped perfectly up to his butt. When he smiled at me I felt weak and extremely pretty at the same time. He wooed me, made me feel like I was the only one for him. He was feeding off my innocence, but even as I grew older this was the type of boy I fell for over and over again: the master manipulator, gaining my attention to use me for their own purpose, and then dropping me in the dirt. I would beg them to stay, because I was on a toxic merry-go-round of low self-esteem, alcoholism, and the inability to say no, because I hoped that if I said yes enough times, one day the merry-go-round would stop.

It was this path of self-destruction that led to the loss of my virginity. I was hanging out at the unit Slash rented with his mate Bumble. On one particular afternoon, Erin was there too, we were watching a movie. I was sitting as close to Slash as I felt I could get while still acting like the young lady my parents wanted me to be. Erin and her boyfriend went into one of the bedrooms. Slash started kissing me, then he took my hand lead me into the same room as our friends. "You guys don't mind us coming in do you?" he asked the others. They shook their heads.

Slash led me to the bed, and we lay down. I watched him take off his watch. Then he rolled over and touched my breasts. He removed my undies, fingered me lightly then entered me. I felt a sharp pain, then the rhythm of his penis. He came and rolled back over. I got up and put on my clothes. Erin got up from the floor where she had been with her boyfriend, and we left together. It was not what I had expected to happen. I had never imagined that I would lose my virginity in that way. There were no declarations of undying love; it was all quite unromantic.

I left without realising Slash had made a bet with his mates that he could take my virginity. I was not as special as

Mother's Day

I thought I was. After that, he became distant and aloof with me. I felt ashamed, shattered and alone. He came to a party at Erin's house, I was excited to see him until I overheard him tell one of his mates that he had enough of me, and that if his mate wanted me, he would be happy for me to go with him. I went out with that boy thinking I would make Slash jealous, but he couldn't care less. He left a giant hole in my heart that I continued to fill with alcohol.

ELIZA JANE

My Darling Charlie,

Do you think the number thirteen is a magical number that makes everyone feel different? Did your life change at the age of thirteen like mine did?

I know my life was changing when you were on the brink of teenage-hood. Did you feel it, or did I hide it from you? I have always worried that you were affected by my breakdown that started at that time in your life.

My thirteenth year was thrown into turmoil by my parents' heated divorce and ensuing custody battle. This was a heart-breaking time in my life, they tried to protect me and my siblings from the full force of it, but I felt it all, saw the anger and hatred. I never wanted you to feel that way about your dad and myself. I wanted you to be able to have two parents who could at least be in the same house together, who could still have a civil conversation when they needed to.

Did your dad and I fight? Yes, we did, I wanted you to see us being adults who did not hide our problems from you like my parents had done to me, until they could no longer keep it a secret. I hope it was easier for you, seeing us working through our issues more openly, not letting things fester.

Teenage years are hard enough to cope with, without our world as we know it caving in around us. I felt it was my responsibility to take charge of the household when Mum became a sole parent. Was it the same for you? Is this why you always thought you had to be the parent in our house, that you did not want me to feel the full responsibility of looking after you?

Mother's Day

I have, for most of my life, measured my success of raising you against my own mother's. With each year, each milestone, every bridge we crossed, I contemplated how Mum did it, asking myself how she would have done it. How did she manage bringing up five children at such a young age? I now know how she did it – she did it because she had to, just like I had to, and just like you will, too.

Teenage years are hard to navigate, from both sides – the teenager's, and the parents'. Now that I am a parent and have lived through all the stages of your childhood and youth, I realise that everything I did as a mother was aimed at ensuring you did not have to go through the issues I had to face.

Other than that, when it came to the more sordid aspects of life, I wanted to protect you from everything that was within my power, I am grateful that you did not have to experience the suicide of a family friend, the death of a grandmother, or seeing your mother being raped. I am also extremely grateful that you did not become a lonely, love addicted alcoholic who was so lost that you could not find your way in the world – at least, I hope not.

Of course, nobody gets to grow up without their share of traumas. That is life. However, I am sorry that you had to witness all the different boyfriends and short-lived relationships I had. It is something that I would change if I could.

Charlie, my teenage years consisted of happy times as well, as I hope yours did. There was a lot of laughter, and we had some good times. It was a time of constant change, I now realise, but I never wanted us to change, for our love to change. I never thought it would.

ELIZA JANE

I am learning that the consequences of our actions have grave repercussions, something you would have thought I would have learnt early on. It just shows that I am a bit of a slow learner sometimes. I hope you can come to understand that my intentions were good, and that one day you will forgive me for the things I got wrong.

Love always.
Mum

Mother's Day

Chapter 3

As I progressed into my teens, life was fun-filled, but at the same time it was becoming a bit of a haze, consisting of parties, booze, and boys on the weekends. My schoolwork was suffering, I was only scraping through, possibly because I spent more time hanging out with my friends at Gran's house, which was right behind the school.

During the morning tea break we would often sneak over to Gran's to sit in the sun and smoke cigarettes. Gran never minded, as long as we did not wake her up. She was a night owl, often not going to bed till after midnight and not getting up until ten. Sometimes, we would head down the river and just skip school all together.

Besides hanging out with my friends, I went to Gran's for lunch a couple of times each week. The five of us would take it in turns to have lunch with Gran so she didn't want for company. She always made sure she had scones for us to eat, after we had finished our sandwiches. This rule also applied to our friends, Gran treated them the same, all were welcome. Our visits meant a lot to her, Gran was not past telling a teacher to get off her property if they came to order us back to school.

On other days, my friends and I would head down to the local fish and chip shop at lunchtime to get a couple of dollars' worth of hot chips with barbeque sauce. The chips were divided equally, and we would find a spot away from school to eat them.

School was definitely more of a social get together for me, somewhere I would meet friends and talk about our current boyfriends, to gossip about who was dating who, who was holding the next party, what we were wearing to the Blue Light Disco at the local hall that Friday night.

The discos were big events in our town. We would all get dressed up and head out for the night. The older boys would be out doing laps of the main street and around the local park in their hotted-up cars. Most of the boys had Monaros, but there were a few Toranas and Valiant Chargers as well. I didn't really care about cars but I loved how the young people in our community were all drawn as one into the centre of town. We would go into the disco to meet our friends and sing the night away, or else we would be hiding in a corner pashing our current boyfriend.

I often spent the weekend at my friend Lilly's house. This meant jumping on the V-line train at Murray and getting off at Gunyah, the next stop down the line. One Saturday Lilly and I headed to Gunyah for the afternoon, she had to work at the local take away shop that evening, so Mum was going to pick me up on her way home from Stoney. We jumped on the train without buying tickets, and as we approached the station we realised the train was not stopping. We had to make a split-second decision as to whether to stay on the train or get off. Lilly's dad was strict; we were scared to call and ask him to come get us from the next town, so we decided to jump. Lilly went first, scraping her hand. I waited for a few seconds before I jumped, but I was inexperienced at train-jumping and, instead of running in the direction the train was headed, I tried coming to a full stop. I tripped and slid across the end of the platform on my chest before tumbling through the air. I remember opening my eyes to see the station master yelling at us for being so stupid.

Lilly helped me up and we went to her house to examine the damage. I had gravel rash from the top of my chest down to my knees, I was having difficulty breathing and was becoming lightheaded. When Mum picked me up later that afternoon she started laughing when I told her what I had done, she could not be angry because she was just so relieved I was alive. She took me into the hospital to make sure I was okay. My one moment of daring turned out to be a week of agony – I had cracked my sternum and given myself a concussion. After the nurse wheeled me into the ward, I imagined I saw my dead Nanna in the bed next to me. It probably was her, wanting to scold me for being such a silly girl.

❖

Monday mornings found us back in class talking about what had happened over the weekend, comparing love bites and holding each other's hands if there was any trouble. My concentration level varied, depending on how interested I was in the subject matter. I assumed I would be one of those kids who breezed through without putting in much effort, after all, I had grand plans of making heaps of money and travelling the world when I grew up. I was going to meet the man of my dreams; we would get married and live happily ever after, why did I even need an education? It was more fun hanging out with my friends and talking about stuff that was extremely important at the time, writing notes to each other, etching our boyfriend's names into the tabletops, and daydreaming about that boy that we secretly had a crush on but whom we dared not ask out.

I always looked forward to Friday night that the Blue Light Disco. My friends and I carefully planned what we were going to wear and how we would do our hair. I could never get my fringe as big as Erin's was, no matter how I tried. My blonde hair was bulky and unmanageable, the cowlick never sat perfectly. As much as I tried, I was hardly what you would call a girly girl. In general, I preferred to be in my jeans riding my pushbike and getting dirty rather than putting on a dress and crimping my hair, much to Gran's disgust.

Regardless of my own preferences, I was desperate to be part of the crowd, so I would put on my prettiest outfit, apply my makeup, do my hair. I had a part time job in a local take-away shop so could afford to buy myself nice clothes, meaning I could disregard the hand-me-downs from my older cousins.

One Friday night I was doing the usual laps of the hall, talking to everyone I knew, watching what was going on, dancing with my friends between smoke breaks outside. I was getting a drink when I bumped into a kid I had never seen. He turned around to look at me and I was mesmerised; he was so tall and handsome and had dark wavy hair. He introduced himself as Todd, the son of a canola farmer, he did not come into town much, never went to the discos either, had only came out that night to make his mates happy.

Todd brought me a Coke and asked me to go out with him the following Friday night.

Mother's Day

After that, Todd took me out regularly for dinner. He bought me jewellery and made me feel incredibly special. He was perfect in my mother's eyes; polite and well mannered, so when he asked if he could take me out to his family farm, she immediately said yes, even though she had banned me from going there previously with Slash because of the wild partying that went on. Mum thought I would be safe now because Todd was a good kid in her eyes, not like the bad boys I had liked to hang out with. This was a sign of trust in me too, it was a sign that our mother-daughter relationship was on the improve.

It was through Todd that I met Jessie, the boy who got me stoned for the first time, and who eventually became the father of my only child. I did not enjoy the feeling of being stoned, it made me want to sleep, unless I had English assignments, when it helped me to produce my best work. I was a cigarette smoker, but the bong made me cough and splutter. I thought I was cool joining in with what everyone else was doing, but drinking was my thing, it seemed like more fun, not that I remembered much due to the blackouts that were happening much more frequently.

I often saw Jessie asleep on the couch at Todd's brother's house, in just his jeans, no shirt showing his bare chest and his tattoo of the devil on his arm. He would sometimes wake up, and while watching us with his steel blue eyes through his naturally curly fringe, he would pack the bong. Then he'd take a long deep breath in as he inhaled the smoke, making the water sound like it was boiling. After he blew out the bong with a lop-sided smile, he would go back to sleep.

At the time I was noticing Jessie, my relationship with Todd was beginning to become strained. He loved me a lot more than I loved him. Had I not been drinking so much I might have made better choices, but I was losing control of myself and had no idea as to what was happening around me.

I broke up with Todd every Thursday because I knew I would drink myself into doing something bad and I didn't like to hurt him. I even begged his parents to order him to leave me alone, but every Monday he would show up at my house and we would get back together.

Beau was still coming to Murray most weekends to visit my friend Ursula. I was jealous of the attention he was giving her, even though I knew I would never go out with him because of the promise I had made to Grant. Beau was clearly unhappy with my drunken antics and would often scold me like a child for my behaviour. I felt bitter and betrayed by his words even though I knew I was being a brat.

My outrageous behaviour was becoming extreme. By the time I reached the age of eighteen, I knew there was something wrong with me. I knew I shouldn't drink, but I didn't know how to stop. As I prepared for the VCE exams I tried to limit the amount of alcohol I was consuming, determined to drink only at certain times on special occasions, but, once I got that first drink into me, I blacked out and all my good intentions went out the window. Due to my lack of preparation, I failed to obtain the VCE, but I did okay in English and Art.

❖

Not long before my eighteenth birthday I had my second encounter with the spirit world. Mum asked me to get a script filled for Pop one afternoon after school. I was full of life as Lynda, my sister and I raced home, but as we walked through the door, we both suddenly felt quite drained, so we decided to have a sleep. At 5.30 I woke up, thirty minutes after the chemist closed. I was so worried, I knew Pop needed his medication, and Mum would be angry with me. She was cross when she arrived home, but nothing could be done; she would get it done the next day.

Mum had not visited her father on her way home from work that day like she usually did. The next day the district who visited Pop called Mum to say she had found him in his favourite chair with his beer alongside him. She was too late to do anything; he had already passed, the time of death showed it was that same afternoon I was supposed to take his script. I am sure now that Nanna was making sure that we were not the ones to find her husband's body. She was an extraordinarily strong woman in life, and she was certainly making her presence felt in the afterlife as well.

I heard the news about Pop from Todd, who was about to have a driving lesson with Mum when she received the call. Mum had gone straight over to Pop's place, leaving Todd to pass on the message. He held me in his arms, at first I did not want to believe it, then I blamed myself - I was responsible, because I had not gone to the chemist and taken him his medicine. I might have saved him, I thought, as I ran to his house. In another part of my brain, I was hoping Todd was wrong, that it was all a mistake, that Pop would be there to greet me as usual when I arrived.

It was true; he was no longer there. The house felt empty and lifeless. My beloved grandparents, who lit up every party were no longer with me.

ELIZA JANE

The weight of the world seemed to shift heavier onto my shoulders. I sank deeper into my sorrows that seemed to be never ending. I found yet another excuse to get drunk and try to forget my troubles. I didn't stop to think that it was Pop's time to go, and that it had not mattered that I did not get to the chemist that day.

Life was becoming a blur; days were melting into each other as I struggled to cope with the loss of my grandfather. I put on a happy face and act cheerful even though I didn't feel like it most days. I felt hollow and empty, like I was on the outside of my body watching everything that was going on, not really taking anything in. I was numb.

My mother spoke to her siblings about buying her parents' house so that we could finally have some permanency in our lives. She used her share in the house to secure a loan so she could pay out the others. We were finally able to move into the one house that had always been a permanent fixture in our lives. Moving here gave me a sense of peace, which I needed more than ever.

❖

I was excited to move to my grandparents' house in the weeks before my eighteenth birthday. It had a large yard where I could celebrate together with my friend Andy. Andy's birthday was the day before mine, but he was turning twenty-two. We went halves in a keg, even though he was not much of a drinker. Unfortunately, this was a good way of masking just how much I was drinking. The day of the party started out well and I waited until after lunch to have my first glass. By six pm I had consumed a full cask of

Lambrusco and was already very drunk by the time it got dark.

After dark, it was like the lights had been turned off and my blackout curtains had come down, only opening a little occasionally, like when a soft breeze is blowing, allowing light flashes of memory: my mother putting me in the shower fully dressed to try and sober me up, going back outside dripping wet to get another drink, everyone pouring their drinks into my cup, leaving the party and going to Kunga across the border in New South Wales where a club stayed open into the small hours of the morning. I remember telling the bouncers it was my eighteenth birthday and that I should be allowed in. It turned out telling the truth was a big mistake. I had been getting into the club for most of the year as an underage kid with a fake ID I had ordered from Queensland. I was not allowed back in until I got real ID.

Unable to get into the club, I left my friends, made my way around to a guy's house that I had been seeing between my on-off relationship with Todd.

When I awoke the next day not remembering how I got home, I knew that I had crossed a line. Andy had been in a fight protecting my honour. I did not remember why, but I was told I had hooked up with a guy who was not Todd. The guilt washed over me; it came up from the pit of my stomach like vomit. Todd told me that was it, I couldn't remember what I did or said that night to make his mind up, but I knew it was true. Remorse and shame flooded my body. My mother was furious with me, I had upset my friends as well, it was like I was living inside a house of cards and it was all falling on top of me.

ELIZA JANE

I broke Todd's heart. To this day he still loathes me for what I did that night, I lost the trust and respect of his family, lost respect for myself. I was a lost, messed-up girl who was quickly spiralling out of control.

I broke the last bit of respect Beau had for me as well that night. I knew that our friendship was at an end now, because I lost the bracelet he had given me for my sixteenth birthday. Whenever we had had a fight in the past, I would lose the bracelet, finding it again only when we were back on track. This time there was little hope that I would find it. I lost my friendship with Ursula as well, as she and Beau were now married and expecting their first child, I was barred from contacting either of them. My protector, my big brother was no longer in my corner and I felt so very alone.

❖

After my birthday, most of that summer was spent in blackout. I was drinking myself into oblivion every night. One night I did not go out with my friends, I was feeling sorry for myself so I decided to stay home where I thought I would get into less trouble. Sitting by myself watching TV I was still able to consume a 700ml bottle of bourbon, and had started on another when my friends came home to find me passed out on the couch. They told me in the morning that I was drinking almost straight alcohol with only a dash of coke. My mother was pulling her hair out at my antics, I did not realise the ripple effect I was causing. I was oblivious, I had no idea what I was doing. I was staying out all night and sleeping through the day.

Mother's Day

Every time I went out I promised myself that this time it would be different; this time I would not get drunk. I ate all my tea before I went out, the theory being that it would be harder to get as drunk on a full stomach, and that I would just have a couple of drinks and everything would okay. Then, every morning I would wake up with a hangover, wondering what I had done the night before.

I knew I was allowing myself to be taken advantage of by the Murray town boys, and losing what little was left of my self-respect in the process. Often I was not even aware of what was happening until it was too late, I would be too sick or too drunk to tell them to stop. After it was over, I would just get up and go home. Each time it happened, the boy concerned would tell me he would meet me next weekend, he would even call through the week and say how he was looking forward to seeing me again, only to message at the last moment that he needed to cancel. Or I would arrive at the designated place, and wait until I realised he was not going to show.

My parents talked me into doing Year 12 again, it was either that, or I was to get a job. I had no idea I wanted to do with my life and thought it was safer to go back to school to give me a better chance.

❖

As I began Year 12 Round Two, I tried to scale back my drinking so I could concentrate on my schoolwork, but my resolve did not last very long. A couple of weeks into the school year saw me back to old habits. I was quickly spiralling out of control again.

ELIZA JANE

I was seeing a boy called Gary for a few weeks when he said he would meet me at the pub at seven o'clock. I showed up on time in a pretty dress and waited, and waited, talking to the other patrons, acting like I was just out having fun and that everything with Gary was fine. As the night went on so did my drinking. The more drinks I had the sadder I became, especially when it became obvious to everyone that I had been dumped again. I should have gone home and cried myself to sleep, like real sober girls do, but I was not sober and now I was a bag of raging emotions.

This pattern continued, and each time I promised myself I would not let it happen again.

It was easy to get a drink in Murray, and when the pubs closed there, we could go across the river to New South Wales and keep drinking there. Now that I had proper ID I was allowed back in and I always ended up there, because it would be open until three am in the morning. I always stayed until closing time even though Mum's curfew was midnight. I was so well known that as soon as the barman saw me coming through the front door, he had my favourite drink waiting for me by the time I made it to the bar, a VB stubby with a dash of lime cordial.

One night I headed over the river to see who was there. I told Mum I was meeting Gary, and I hoped to, I still hadn't given up on him even though he had made any contact after the night he stood me up. All too soon I was drowning my sorrows once again. I had a hollow feeling deep in my stomach, I felt like the world had moved on and left me behind. The club was packed and noisy. I was wandering around, drink in hand talking to everyone I knew and looking happy, when I spied Jessie. I couldn't see that he was with anyone. We began talking. I remember him kissing me, and him coming home with me.

The next morning, my mother lost her temper, dragged me into the laundry to tell me off for bringing Jessie home, yelling at me about how I had gone out the night before to meet Gary, only to come home with Jessie.

I tried explaining what happened, but in hindsight it was easy to see she had enough of my drunkenness, my total irresponsibility, and my disregard for my younger siblings.

Jessie called a mate to come and get him. He told me he was going away for his brother's wedding the following weekend that he would call me when he came back. I doubted he would, he was probably just like his mates who had passed me round already. I considered that he had even been dared by a mate to see if he could get into my pants. So many thoughts went through my head, but for some reason I stopped dwelling on Jessie and got on with my life.

I was surprised to see him when, two weeks later, he turned up at our house on his motor bike. I invited him in. I was sceptical and intrigued at the same time. There was something about Jessie something that drew me.

Because I had not even considered Jessie would come back, I had already decided by then that I needed to move in with Dad and Penny in Bloom. I was desperate to try and curb my drinking and firmly believed I would be able to do it if I were living with Dad. I was still ashamed to drink around him, it felt like a betrayal, after all he had been through to become sober. I still did not really understand why I felt the need to hide it, and I still did not know why Dad had given up alcohol, but I thought that if I were living there, I would be less tempted to drink. I hated the thought of disappointing him, and I did not want to take the shine off being daddy's little girl. It seemed like a solid plan.

Bloom was around a four-hour drive from Murray, on the coast. Over the previous summer I had a job there while I stayed with Dad and Penny, not far from Malus where I had started high school. I worked in a convenience store, which was a great way to make money, but it was hard work. Dad picked me up on my first day and told me to go back in and ask my boss if I could work more hours. I worked from eight in the morning until two in the afternoon, then I was back from four till eleven pm, seven days a week. After five weeks of long hours with no days off I was more than happy to go back to school. Now in danger of failing Year 12 a second time, Mum, Dad and I all thought it would be best if I went back to the coast to finish the VCE, far away from temptation.

The move did not eventuate. When I told Jessie about the plan, he told me that he did not want me to move so far away. He wanted to go out with me. I was stunned, but we were kindred spirits. Our love of drinking certainly bonded us. We took each other hostage. I stayed.

I moved into my grandparents' old caravan that was in our backyard. It was Mum's solution, to stop me from continuing to be a bad influence on my younger siblings, as well as creating a space for me to start learning to live on my own while she was close enough to protect me if needed. I could also get my schoolwork done in peace. Jessie never took me out on dates, we just went to the pub for a drink. That, along with sex were the two things we shared.

For a few weeks I was very content. I felt happy and safe in a relationship for the first time. However, with me, feeling content usually lasted for only a small period of time. One day Jessie called me to tell me he was on his way to North Queensland to work with his dad. I was shattered. He did not come to tell me himself, he just left. I thought that was it, he would not come back. I felt angry and betrayed. I hung up the phone in the hallway, removed a clip from my hair and threw it as hard as I could towards the back door, narrowly missing my mother who was coming into the kitchen. With tears streaming down my face, I ran past her to the caravan and cried huge tears into my pillow.

The next morning, I apologised for my behaviour. Mum hugged me, smoothed my hair back and reassured me that everything would be ok. I got on with life again, trying to concentrate on my schoolwork.

❖

Jessie was calling regularly from North Queensland, talking about his work on the farm with his dad, how they were staying in a house on a property that was fully set up for people who needed somewhere to stay as they passed by. It was in the middle of nowhere. My nerves were temporarily quietened, I felt hope again.

Jessie was away for about six weeks when he rang me to tell me he was on his way home. I was so excited, the Easter school holidays were approaching. He hitch-hiked all the way, and during the last stretch of his journey we were both listening to Motley Crue's new song, 'Home Sweet Home'; it became our song. I did not want him to leave my side, I wanted him to myself, but he went out drinking with his mates, and did not turn up when he said he would. It made me paranoid.

There were so many red flags that I chose to ignore. I should have walked away at that point, but it was like we were addicted to each other, I had not learnt yet that people need space, and I was incredibly clingy.

The Easter holidays started soon after Jessie came home, which gave me time to put the schoolbooks away and concentrate on him, on us. One night after we had been out drinking, we made love in my cosy little van. Afterwards, my instinct told me I was pregnant. I dismissed it at the time, but six weeks later we were standing in Mum's hallway having 'the talk'. Mum had already guessed. I knew without a doubt that I was going to keep the baby.

I gave Jessie a choice, to either stay and be a dad or to leave and never come back. He chose to stay, much to my relief. It was a lot for us to take in, we had only been seeing each other for a couple of months. The plan was that I would stay in Murray to finish school, while he would go back to Queensland where there were more jobs.

I told Dad over the phone, which was the easiest way. I knew I had let him down, he expected so much more from me and was already disappointed with the gossip he was hearing about me from the people in Murray. To their credit, while my parents were not overly happy about my being pregnant, they were both supportive – while making it clear that the baby was my responsibility, not theirs. I felt ready to take on the challenges of being a parent, and excited at the idea of having someone in my life who would love me unconditionally.

I continued with my schooling, hoping to finish Year 12. On reflection, I should have left when I found out I was pregnant, because by the time exams started I had baby brain and did not really care whether I passed or not. I just wanted to be a mother, living the happy family life I believed we would always have, this was something I had craved ever since my parents' split. I thought, too, that a family of my own would give me something else to focus on, which in turn would help me to stop drinking.

Early into my first trimester, Jessie went to Queensland to work as a mechanic in a place called Karinga. He was unqualified, but he was one of those blokes that could turn his hand to anything he wanted to do. He rang me every day, usually after he had been to the pub, sounding very drunk and always professing his love for me. Once, after I hung up and went to bed, he woke up the next day with the phone still on his lap.

I visited for the first time in the winter school holidays. Jessie met me at the airport. I felt like I was in a movie, coming down the escalator into the arms of the man who would look after me for the rest of my life. The next morning, I woke early to call Mum from a payphone so she would know I had arrived safely. It was a hilly area, and as I got to the top of the road, I stopped on the corner of the street to look out over the tops of the houses towards the sprawling city in front of me. I was quickly falling in love with the subtropical warmth, and I was already feeling lighter, being far away from Murray.

By the end of that year, I found I had not done any better in my exams than the year before, but at least this time I was not drunk for the entire year. When I had found out I was pregnant, I had made a conscience decision to curb my drinking and smoking for the baby's health.

Four days after I turned nineteen, seven months pregnant, I was ready to leave home and begin family life in Queensland. Excitement mounted as I bought my ticket on a Greyhound bus, it was all I could afford, and it was an exceptionally long trip, taking nearly twenty-four hours. It was a road that I would travel many times, but the first trip was special, because I was leaving home for the first time. My parents came with me to the bus stop, and as I looked through the window and waved, I saw Dad crying next to the petrol pump – it is an image that will never leave me. As I left for my new adventure – not only motherhood, but a new city and state too – I did not know then just how young and naïve I was, wearing my rose-coloured glasses.

Mother's Day

My Darling Charlie,

I was just fifteen when I first tasted alcohol, and I loved how it made me feel. I felt like I was a whole new person, I came out of my shell, felt confident getting out and exploring the world around me. It wasn't till later that I realised that even at that early age I was already in the grip of the dark side of alcoholism. Blackouts happened every time I drank. I was surprised at how quickly my drinking crept up and spiralled out of control, I knew by the age of eighteen there was something wrong with the way I drank, I just did not know how to stop.

I wasted my high school years on booze and low self-esteem.

When you were in high school, I prayed that you would get through it without all the drama that I had brought on myself. Of course, I knew there would be romances and experimentation with alcohol in your life. Do you remember how I reacted to the first time you got drunk? I was worried but reserved judgement as I knew it was a rite of passage. I just wanted you to concentrate on your schooling. I wanted you to do better than me, as every parent wants for their child. And you did, I think that by the time you were sixteen you already had a plan formulated in your head as to what you wanted in life. You were already pushing for that to happen regardless of what I thought about it.

You may have felt I was not always there for you during your teenage years. I was fighting with depression, but I kept working to keep a roof over our heads and to maintain some stability in your life, so I ignored my own health issues. It was easier to stay busy than to stop. You were the reason that I kept going, making sure you were getting what you needed.

I might not have always been physically available, but I was always with you within my heart. Mentally, too, my head was not there, and I was working so very hard to halt the dark clouds that had descended on my life. I was fighting against change, against you growing up and becoming independent, when you would no longer need me, and against the knowledge that I needed to do something to help myself. Maybe I should have just given into it and let out all the pain I was so carefully keeping hidden.

But, if I had given in, I might not be here to write this.

Love always.
Mum

Chapter 4

Waking up every day to warm weather and sunshine was bliss. It warmed my soul, I felt like I was in a new world, a haven of sorts. I was completely anonymous in my new world as well, there was no way that my parents could keep an eye on me, they were thousands of kilometres away. Even though I spoke to Mum most days and Dad weekly, I needed to still feel connected to them, just without the apron strings.

Without my large family and the town of Murray where everyone knew what everyone else was doing. It felt strange that I could come and go as I pleased. I loved exploring my new city. I loved being a housewife and doing the washing and the cooking. The freedom was intoxicating.

We were staying in the boarding house that Jessie had been living in since he arrived. We had a good-sized room and shared the rest of the house with the Hungarian owner who loved to play the tuba when he thought nobody was around. The house was not a traditional Queenslander, but in Queensland style it was built high off the ground. I was amazed at how small the boundary fences were, everyone could see into each other's yards. This was something I was not used to. In Victoria we had had high fences to keep out the neighbours.

ELIZA JANE

Frank, our landlord introduced me to the tropical fruit of Queensland that he grew in his garden. I was not a fan of pawpaw or avocados, but I loved mangos and macadamia nuts. The house was within walking distance of the train and bus, making it easy to head to the city to explore places like the art gallery and museum, and for getting my bearings around the local area.

Before I left Murray, my doctor had given me a list of things to do to prepare for the birth. At the top of the list was finding a hospital. One Saturday, while Jessie and I were out looking at potential rentals in nearby suburbs, I spotted a hospital. It was a hot and humid day and we had probably already walked for a least ten kilometres, neither of us had our driver's licence (even though Jessie drove illegally), and we did not have access to a car. As we walked through the main entrance of the hospital, I found a nurse and asked if this was a maternity hospital. I was huffing and puffing and sweating profusely and she immediately thought I was in labour, I reassured her that I was just in a need of a drink of water. She sighed with relief and explained that for a maternity ward I would need to go to the Terra, a public hospital in the city, and make inquiries.

The following Monday morning I dressed in my best maternity clothes and caught the train into the city. I had worked out which station I needed to get off, and the station master gave me directions to the hospital.

On arrival I asked at the main reception about booking myself in to give birth and was told I would need to see my doctor. I smiled brightly and said that was impossible as my doctor was in Victoria. The nurse took down all my details, and I left with a list of weekly appointments with an obstetrician right there at the hospital.

It felt like a dream, waking up each day excited about becoming a parent. Jessie was not quite so happy about the idea of being a father though, and I started to see a different side of him – often nasty, especially when he was drunk. I tried to ignore his taunts which was a hard thing to do, especially as he made me cry most days. The thing that hurt the most was that he quickly became jealous of our growing baby. He told me once he did not want me to have the baby, because he did not want to share me with anyone. I thought it would be different when the baby was born and put it down to the nerves of being a first-time parent.

Jessie was a man of few words; he liked to keep his thoughts private, while being a keen observer of people and their actions. No one ever really knew Jessie, not even me. I was surprised when I learnt that he had not told anyone in Karinga I was coming, nor that we were expecting our first child. Frank was unaware of my pregnancy until the day he found me slumped on the floor in the hallway in the middle of a dizzy spell, which I later found out was a form of headache caused from stress. His concern about me quickly turned to surprise when I had told him about my condition. I would have thought that in the almost seven months Jessie had been living there he would have at least told Frank, but no, he hadn't said a word.

Jessie and I spent our first Christmas in the share house. I was surprised when I realised Jessie had not thought about buying me a Christmas present until he discovered I had brought him one. At the last minute, he went out and bought me a new hairdryer. It was not very romantic, but it was useful. It lasted for twelve years.

I eventually found a house for us all to live in not far from the boarding house. We moved in just after New Year's Eve, thinking there would be plenty of time.to set it up before the baby arrived. Each week I looked through the *Trading Post* for second-hand furniture and on weekends we would go and look at the things I had marked out. I would also find things at the local op shop. I was not afraid of exploring, one day I had seen a notice for an auction at a local pub. I took the bus but got off too early and ended up walking for a couple of kilometres uphill in the middle of the day, just to buy saucepans. Being heavily pregnant made it slow going.

Mum come to stay with us in the week leading up to the due date. She and I explored second-hand stores around the city and surrounding suburbs, and together we set up the nursery. With the baby keeping it a secret as to the actual time of their arrival, Mum returned home just before the Australia Day long weekend, to rescue my brothers and sisters from each other.

There were moments in my pregnancy when Jessie was very attentive, showing his kind and loving side. On Australia Day he suggested we go into the city to see the fireworks. I was delighted to discover he had arranged for some people he knew from the pub to come along with us. That day I met Ruby, Amanda, and Grace, never expecting to see them again, but I was happy to have the company, as there was little chance to meet anyone. I felt a little shy as I was extremely pregnant and due to give birth that day; I drank more than I should that night.

Mother's Day

Dad and Penny arrived the next day. They stayed at a local hotel but came over every day to help get things ready for the birth. Jessie and I were incredibly happy that they had not been here at the same time as Mum, there was still so much animosity between my parents.

My cousin Lizzy, who lived close by, would often visit with her young son. I invited her and her family over for her birthday dinner, the baby was already a week overdue by then. I emptied out the toybox so the little boy had some things to play with, but not being used to toys on the floor, I tripped on a little car and needed to steady myself so I did not fall. The jolt was enough to make the baby to decide it was time to come out and meet us.

ELIZA JANE

My Darling Charlie,

Those last few months before you were born were the happiest, I have ever known.

I was happy to be living far away from Murray, and to finally be able to stand on my own two feet, even if I was wobbly at times as we all are when we are thrust into adulthood. I loved learning how to do things like shopping and paying bills, even though it was Jessie's money that paid the bills back then and not my own. I enjoyed looking after the house and getting out every day, exploring the new city. Nanna had said Brisbane was like a big country town, and she was right. It was big and friendly and easy to navigate. I felt confident and free.

I would often place my hands on my bulging stomach and talk to you. I would ask you what you were going to look like. I would tell you how much I loved you and that you would never want for anything in this world. At the same time, I was anxious of how my life was going to be as a parent, your dad was already showing signs of a lack of responsibility, even before you were born. I tried to ignore his snide remarks that I thought were due to nervousness at the prospect of becoming a father. He made me feel like I was never doing things the right way, he wanted me to do everything the way his mother did and it made me unsure of myself. I wanted to do things the way my own mother had done when I was growing up. Was this wrong? I do not know; I was so in love with your dad that I wanted him to always be happy, regardless of whether it made me happy or not.

Mother's Day

Have you followed in your dad's footsteps or mine when it comes to the way you live your life? I see both Jessie and I in you. You look a lot like me, and I think I passed on my strength to you. Though I sense through your silence that there is a lot of Jessie in you, too. Is this what is keeping you from communicating with me? Did you inherit your father's stubborn sullen nature? I hope there is at least a small part of your life that you are willing to share.

I am so looking forward to seeing you as a parent one day, and me as a grandmother — but don't do it while you are young, like I did!

Love always.
Mum

Chapter 5

I woke early the morning after my cousin's birthday dinner. As I ran my hand over my bulging stomach to feel the baby moving, I could tell the birthing process had begun. It felt like the unborn infant was swinging off my ribs as it turned itself around to get into position. As much as I would have liked to stay in bed, I had to get up, I could feel pain at the bottom of my back. The waterbed, which I would never recommend for a pregnant woman to sleep in, was cold against my back. When Jessie rolled over to give me a morning cuddle, I gave him a kiss and told him he was going to be a father that day.

As I was getting up, I could already feel that it was going to be a warm summer's day, the humidity was making everything feel sticky, and it was only six am.

I was still getting used to the heat. It was so different from the dry Victorian summer; Queensland weather leaves you feeling exhausted and slightly sick, until the summer storm hits around three pm, cooling everything down. Until I moved here, I had never stood under so many cold showers in the attempt to stop my body sweating.

After a glass of cold water and a shower, I felt restless and uncomfortable but did not know what to do with myself. The morning stretched out in front of me; I walked around the house, taking notice of everything in it. It was a funny little house, with only two bedrooms and no proper internal doors, each of the bedrooms had double swinging doors that had no handles or locks. Our bedroom did not even have a window or a light as it was right in the centre in of the house. The baby's room had a little window above the cot. Both bedrooms opened onto a sunroom, making it easy to walk in a circle around the inside of the house.

The two bedrooms were connected by a wardrobe which would make it easy for me to hear the baby from our room – whenever it decided to arrive. I originally wanted to co-sleep, but Jessie pointed out it was not good for the baby's emotional growth, arguing that I would be close enough if we left the wardrobe doors open. I relented, agreeing that this was a sensible solution.

As I circled the house, I thought about what my unborn child would look like? What sort of person would they be? Would I be a good mother? So many thoughts go through your head when you are waiting, and many fears too. Jessie had banned me from watching the midday movies that always seemed to be about child kidnappings or deaths, it freaked me out and he had to calm me down each night when he came home from work. My imagination was too vivid for his liking.

I did not wonder what sex my baby would be, I guessed before I even had the scan. My spirit world, or my female intuition told me I was pregnant the night I conceived and told me the sex of the baby too. I have chosen not to reveal the gender because it does not matter, since the first moment of conception I knew I loved my child and will continue to do so unconditionally for the rest of my life.

ELIZA JANE

❖

Jessie and I had already picked the name, which was made up using the names of other people we loved. Some had left us and were watching over our baby from beyond the clouds, they were strong and fierce just like I hoped my baby would grow up to be. I knew they would all have loved my baby just as much as I already did.

Dad and Penny arrived later in the morning to spend the day with me. Dad was like an expectant new father as he watched me moving around restlessly, he could tell when the pains were coming. I am sure he felt every one of my contractions like they were his own, but he never said anything. He filled in the hours drinking endless cups of coffee, making jokes, and helping Jessie work on a car. Over the course of the day I often caught him watching me with great love and pride in his eyes.

The day stretched from dawn to dusk, my legs were hurting, my back was sore from standing. If I tried to sit down or thought about stretching out on the couch, I couldn't stay put for long. I was just too excited. I can't remember eating or drinking much, but I am sure I would have had a bag of radishes at some time during the day as this was all I craved throughout my pregnancy. I know Penny would have fed me and made sure I was okay.

During those final hours before we left to go to the hospital the baby was becoming more restless, moving around to get into position. Other than the pain of each contraction, I felt very calm, I had no fear or anxiety at the thought of what was going to happen, there was just a rare and wonderful tranquillity.

Mother's Day

The time finally came for Jessie and me to head off to the hospital. It was around six pm, I had been on my feet for twelve hours and was more than ready for the baby to come out. In preparation for this day, we had done a few practice runs to the hospital to work out the best route. This time it was a bit more urgent, and a lot more anxiety-ridden, especially as it was peak hour on a Friday evening. We did not talk much, Jessie was concentrating on getting to the hospital in one piece while I had a chance to watch the sun setting over the hills and see the sky's peach glow, indicating it would rain the next day. As we turned into the hospital, we were just two young people who were scared about what was about to happen and excited at the same time.

The birthing suite was a large room, it was not what I had expected, I thought we would have shared with someone, but we had the whole room to ourselves. As I was helped onto the bed the pain was getting more intense and the contractions were coming closer and closer. I never imagined there would be this much pain. The nurse asked me if I wanted an epidural, I declined, though I did ask for pain relief closer to the time, only to be told it was too late. I later found out that the epidural was a large needle. I am glad I refused, I have a fear of needles and I might have screamed on seeing it and finding out where it would have gone.

I was a little scared of what was going on, I did not really have any idea what childbirth was all about. The doctor was young, and this was his first birth too, so he was inexperienced. I became annoyed with his constant advice; he was probably nervous himself and was just trying to be helpful. I imagine I said some things that were not nice, but I did apologise afterwards.

ELIZA JANE

Jessie and I were completely unprepared. We had no idea about antenatal classes - which would have helped, but all I had learned was things Mum told me, even then I had not really listened closely, like most teenagers.

As the baby was preparing to come out, I needed to change position constantly to try to get comfortable. I really needed to go to the toilet, but the nurses were scared that I would give birth in there. The pain in my back and abdomen was intense. When the nurses told me to start pushing Jessie stood behind me, my left hand gripped his hand, and my right hand was up behind his neck; each time a new contraction came, I pulled down, not knowing I was hurting him. He did not complain, he didn't say a thing about it until after we came home from the hospital. I think he was as scared as I was, it was quite different watching his own child being born to seeing a lamb begin born on his family's sheep property.

The nurses asked if we wanted a mirror to see the baby's head crowning. At first, I said no, I thought it would look terrible, but I quickly changed my mind when the crown started to come through. Jessie did not want to miss a thing. He watched as his child came into the world, but even though there was a mirror, with the last big push I closed my eyes and missed it.

Jessie cut the umbilical cord before they put the crying infant on my chest. I counted ten little fingers and ten little toes. We felt a sense of awe, of pure love for the little creature we had created. Jessie had wanted to video tape the birth, but I would not let him. I wish I had, now.

The nurse cleaned up the baby and did the necessary checks before wrapping our darling child in a blanket to keep warm while they finished cleaning me up. As they brought the baby back to us, the pain and the trauma of giving birth was already forgotten; it felt like it had happened a million years ago, but was probably only twenty minutes.

Jessie said he wanted to extend the middle name, to incorporate more love for those had gone before us, and to those who were still here. I thought it made the name more beautiful, more powerful. When it was time for Jessie to go home, he kissed me and gazed down at the sleeping child in my arms, saying he would see us in the morning. After he was gone, I showered and to put on clean PJs. For the first time in a while, I was able to see my toes.

Cleansed and refreshed, I stood for ages looking down into the crib and wondered how this baby had fitted inside my body. It was overwhelming. When I was taken to the maternity ward it was after ten thirty, and I was exhausted. The nurse took the baby to the nursery for the first few hours for observation, and to give me a chance to rest. I was so tired; I think I was asleep within minutes of arriving in the ward.

I was woken a few hours later by a nurse saying it was time to feed my baby. I sat up in the bed, my small child was handed to me. It all seemed so natural. I watched the little lips pucker around my nipple, feeding from me for the first time. I wondered if I was doing it correctly, but figured it was okay as I felt the let-down. I went back to sleep with the baby on my chest. It was to become our favourite sleeping position in the months to come.

Dad and Penny came to the hospital the next day. It warmed my heart to see Dad looking so proud as he held his first grandchild in his arms. A special bond was formed that day. I asked if they could get me some orange juice from downstairs as I was thirsty; the hospital had only given me a small juice and no water. Dad was unable to contain himself, not only did he bring back my juice, but also a big bunch of flowers, baby clothes and a teddy bear, which was soon christened 'Poppa Bear'.

Jessie and I were so young and naïve, we thought we could do everything we wanted. We had moved away from our families, and now we were a family. We wanted to prove to everyone that we could do it on our own, just like they had.

I thought I was breaking the mould and doing it my way, but I was actually following in my parent's footsteps; I just did not realise how closely I was following. I was not any different, I was just living in a different era.

Mother's Day

My Darling Charlie

What an extraordinary day it was the day you were born. My heart filled with so much love, more than I could have ever expected. I wish I could give birth to you every day and feel that love and sense of wonder again and again.

Being your mother has been my greatest achievement to date, hands down. My darling child it has been a privilege that you chose me to be your parent, even with the heartbreak that you are causing now through your silence. I just pray that this is only a moment in time, a test of my patience and resilience, like all the other tests that have been sent to me.

As I sit here writing this letter, I am remembering the child I was when you come along. I had not learned how to live my own life, I was barely twenty years old myself, and Jessie, your father, was at the tender age of twenty-three. We still had a lot of learning to do, but life does that to you, does it not?

If I could go back and change anything, it would be when I had you. I always wanted to be your mother, I just wish I had first grown up and become more responsible, that I had learned to manage my drinking and had stopped being the party girl. Once I was settled in a stable and loving relationship, not only with your father, but myself as well, then I would have been the mother you felt you needed.

Love always.
Mum

Chapter 6

You were five days old when we went home from the hospital. I did not know then that we could have left earlier. Having been in a large ward with a lot of other mothers and their babies, I was able to learn my child's distinct cries - Jessie presumed I would have known instinctively. There were good things about being in the hospital, but I found it overwhelming. At home I was able to get us both into a routine very quickly. My life revolved around that routine; with a baby there was so much more to do so I focused on making every minute count. I never wanted Jessie to come home to a crying baby or to a messy house with no dinner on the table. He was already nit-picking about what I did and did not do while he was at work.

I worked around the baby's feeding and sleeping times. It did make it easy that I seemed to have the most docile infant on the planet. My little bundle of joy seemed to take after me and could sleep through anything: the vacuum cleaner, television, even music blaring on the stereo.

On shopping days, I would wait till just before nap time to get on the bus and head to the shopping centre; the motion of the moving bus would rock the baby to sleep. I always took the bus that followed the longest route to give both of us some rest. It worked like a charm, I managed to do all the shopping without the worry of a fussy child.

About a week after I came home, Ruby, Amanda and Grace came to meet the baby. I was excited that they wanted to visit, inviting them in and proudly showing them around. Then we sat in the loungeroom and they took turns holding the baby.

The girls became a regular feature in our house. Every weekend they kept me company while Jessie was at the pub. Sometimes they came to the shops, at other times we stayed home and drank wine.

Weekends were easy, but Jessie was going out more and more on weeknights as well, leaving me at home with the baby for long periods of time. I felt alone and frustrated at Jessie's lack of care for us. When the baby was around six weeks old Jessie went to a party, leaving me home again. He said he would not be out for long, that he needed a bit of fun. It was pointless arguing that he was out all the time. I settled in to watch TV, the baby was starting to become a little fussy with feeding, so I did not mind staying in. I wanted to keep breastfeeding as I thought this was the best, but it was tiring. By the time evening came I was often exhausted. Normally I would fall asleep on the couch watching *Star Trek* with the baby asleep on my chest. On that particular night, though, the evening dragged with the baby's cries getting louder, I presumed from hunger. My anxiety grew with each hour that passed: ten pm rolled around, midnight, one am, two am. The baby would only settle for a short time.

At eight am Jessie came home. I was furious and exhausted in equal measure. How dare he stay out all night! He told me he had passed out and had not meant to stay out so long. I looked at him and told him I did not care for his excuses, I needed him to go to the supermarket to get bottles, teats and formula for our hungry baby. He left straight away and was back within a half an hour, but by that time I had been able to get the baby to go to sleep. I stacked everything in a cupboard and finally, utterly exhausted, I slept for most of the day.

I cried as I made up the first bottle because I did not feel like I was being a good mum. I continued trying to breastfeed for another month, mostly in the mornings, until it was clear it was not working.

We took our first trip back to Murray a couple of months after the birth. Jessie had been asked to be a groomsman for a friend's wedding. Excited to go home and show off my baby, I packed our bags, including every cloth nappy that I owned, not thinking to buy disposable nappies or that I might not be able to use Mum's washing machine, and booked our tickets on the Greyhound bus.

I had lost so much weight after the birth and from walking everywhere that I did not have anything to wear to the wedding. A friend of Mum's lent me a size eight dress that was still slightly too large for me.

Mum looked after the baby while we went to the wedding. Because I was not breast feeding any longer, Jessie and I got very drunk. The next morning, I woke up to hear the front door-bell ringing. I answered the door with a dress wrapped around me. I was surprised to see Jessie's dad and a woman standing on the doorstep. I asked him to wait a minute while I got dressed. I closed the door and told Jessie his dad was at the door.

Mother's Day

We quickly dressed and I opened the door to Jessie's dad and his friend. As Jessie shook his father's hand I was surprised to hear him say, "Hello Mum".

Yikes! I had met Jessie's mum for the first time half-dressed and with a terrible hangover!

Mum made coffee for Jessie's parents, Henry and Milly, while I got the baby ready to meet them. They took us to meet Leigh, Jessie's sister, and her husband John. John doted on the baby as he and Leigh were unable to have children of their own. It was my first real induction to Jessie's family. It was nice to see our families, but after a week away I was ready to get back into the routine of our life in Karinga.

The baby was about eight months old when Henry, Jessie's dad, rang from the farm in Cotton, in northern New South Wales, asking for Jessie's help. We talked about it through the day. I did not want Jessie to leave, but if he went, I wanted him to take me and the baby with him. Jessie was firm with me and said I was better off in Karinga, that I could get the single mother's pension and he would spend one week out of every three with us.

I did not like it, but I went along with it when Jessie explained he could make better money for our family if he worked with his dad. It was lonely without Jessie there beside me. He called every day, but I felt sad and empty. During the day, the baby kept me busy, but my drinking was starting to escalate again. In the evenings, I would have a glass of wine with my dinner, put the baby to bed and finish the bottle – or two – before going to sleep myself.

On the weekends I would invite the girls over for drinks so I was not drinking by myself all the time, and to help break up the boredom that would descend over me in the evenings.

Whenever Jessie came home, I was so excited. It was like there was lightness again in the house. I was no longer on my own managing everything. Jessie paid the bills, took me shopping for food and spoiled me with presents. I had a drinking buddy as well, it was something we did every weeknight, as well as having a party on the weekend so he could catch up with all our friends.

Jessie didn't come home nearly as often as he promised, but he was there for the baby's first Christmas. I had a cactus decorated as a Christmas tree with all the presents were under it. His sisters and their husbands, along with Jessie's dad, spent the day with us. It was only our second Christmas together, the first as a family. As we lay in bed talking about what needed to be done before everyone arrived, I began to feel comfortable, it seemed that all was right with the world. What a surprise I got when Jessie rolled towards me and asked me to be his wife. I was so excited, he told me that we would go shopping for an engagement ring after Christmas.

The glamour wore off a little later in the day when we announced that we were engaged. Henry gave a snort of laughter, like he did not believe it. I shook off this moment of unease, but the laughter hung around in my memory, and along with it, a sense of dread.

My Darling Charlie,

Your first year of life seems like such a long time ago, but at the same time it feels like it all happened yesterday. Time moves so quickly when you are not staying in the present but dreaming of a magical future that might never eventuate. Now, I wish I could go back to that time in your life when you loved and needed me. But wishing for things to go back in time is pointless. My life is going on, with or without you in it.

You were such a great baby, you hardly ever cried. You were content to gurgle and babble to yourself as I worked around the house. That was a massive year of learning for me, the responsibility of being a parent and the anxiety of hoping I was doing all the right things weighed heavily. Living a long way away from my parents and family was hard as well. I was always on the phone to Mum or Penny asking for advice. Our phone bill was probably huge, thinking about the number of times I called one or other of them.

Whenever Jessie was away working, my anxiety and alcoholism increased, and soon it reached the point where I was not coping. I sought the help of a doctor, who put it down to baby blues and gave me a prescription for Xanax. My anxiety might have eased if I had stopped drinking as well, but that was never mentioned. It would not be the first time that I would encounter a doctor who was happy to just hand out antidepressants and not look more closely at my lifestyle.

I realise now that I was already a single mother, I had been from the moment you were conceived. Maybe I should have left it that way instead of chasing Jessie to be a partner and a father. Jessie might not have been the best partner, but I will always be grateful to him for three things that happened.

First of all is YOU! You are the best thing that could have happened to either of us. You gave me a purpose in life that I never questioned. Jessie loved you in his own way and he was also very proud of you.

The second thing he gave me: Sobriety! His threat of taking you away from me was the second-best thing to happen to us, because if he had not made me choose between drinking and our family, you would probably have grown up with two alcoholic parents instead of one.

Thirdly, Jessie introduced me to a strong and faithful tribe that surrounded you with love and support while you were growing up. Ruby, Amanda and Grace were amazing friends, especially when I really did become a single parent.

I resented that I was forced to raise you on my own. But I never resented you. I realise now that growing up in such a large family with people constantly around me made me want that for you. I enjoy being a part of a tribe. You are the centre of my life though, not even a hundred people could replace you, and I miss you more than anything Charlie.

There is a big gaping hole in my heart. I need you to know that.

Love always.
Mum

Chapter 7

Was it already a year since I gave birth? The time had disappeared so quickly. I had hoped that Jessie would be home for the first birthday celebrations, but he was still away working. He sent me some money to go shopping to get everything I needed to spoil our baby.

This was a disappointing experience for me, and one that felt so strange after growing up surrounded by a large family. There were no other children, no balloons or party streamers, just a store-bought cake with a one little candle. Fortunately, Ruby, Amanda, and Grace came to help me celebrate this first, and not last milestone in my baby's life.

It was a Friday night, and after we celebrated the birthday and put the baby to bed, we continued to party. For me it was another excuse to have people over so that I did not have to drink alone.

Except for the times I let my hair down, it seemed like every waking minute had been allocated to one thing or another since I had given birth. I loved every minute of being a mother, there was always something new to learn or to discover. Jessie and I adopted a puppy to grow with our baby, and for company for me. There were added bonuses too. I did not need to clean the floor after any meal, I just let the dog in and she would lick it clean. It was also nice to have the security of a dog to protect us if needed, especially now that Jessie was away working most of the time.

I worried like any mother about my child's progress through the early stages, but the nurse at the clinic said I was doing a great job and the baby was healthy and meeting all the required milestones. (She did point out once that I had put the disposable nappy on backwards.)

I enjoyed it when Jessie came home, it freed me up to go out and do things on my own, to have a break from the baby and let them have some bonding time. In true Jessie style though, every time I came home, he would have put the baby in a basket, or played some other practical joke.

Jessie did not seem as excited as I thought he would about achievements like first steps and new teeth coming through. I would often watch from the window to see Jessie playing happily in the yard with our child, until he saw me watching and would quickly halt the game. I saw the happy face of my little child turn to one of distress and dismay as the fun abruptly ceased. It broke my heart; I could not understand why Jessie turned so cold so quickly.

With a toddler on the move my days became even busier. I childproofed the house as much as I thought I could, putting breakable things away and creating a safe play area in the kitchen. I looped bandanas through the handles of the cupboards to prevent the pots and pans banging and clanging, a noise that grew even more offensive through a hangover, which was most days now.

My brothers Peter and Nathan were into everything when they were babies. I did not think I would cope if I had to deal with accidents like my mother had. Peter was forever in the doctor's having multiple stiches, and Nathan would sneak through the window when he was just two years old; Mum would find him having breakfast with the neighbours. I certainly did not want that kind of worry and was always watching closely, hoping nothing bad would happen.

We could not childproof everything though. One day Jessie and I were busy with chores around the house when I realised the house was far too silent, there were none of the usual child-related sounds. We could not even hear the dog barking. My motherly instincts went into overdrive as every possible scenario went through my head while I searched anxiously for the child and the dog. I called Jessie help, and while I went out along our driveway he kept searching the house. I was a frantic, screaming mess, looking up and down the street when I heard Jessie calling my name.

I rushed inside to the kitchen, still with a look of horror on my face, when I saw Jessie was in the laundry. He smiled at me and said, "Wendy it's ok, I found our water baby.". I was confused and still a bit hysterical as I went down the few steps into our laundry to see what he was looking at. Soon I was laughing uncontrollably, Jessie had found our little one wedged into the toilet bowl, dressed from head to toe in rain gear: little red gumboots, matching red pants and a red raincoat, a wide grin from ear to ear. After being released from the toilet bowl, it warmed my heart to see a small finger looped through the dog's collar. She had been sitting faithfully next to my baby for protection, I heard soft baby words spoken that only the dog understood, and a tilt of the dog's head as she followed instructions. My heart filled with love at the sight of the bond that had been formed.

ELIZA JANE

My Darling Charlie,

Loneliness and a sense of abandonment followed me through most days when your dad was away. I thought I was managing as a stay-at-home mum, I told myself my drinking was under control. I was not managing though, and with every word that I write memories are popping into my head of our life back when you were so little and defenceless.

Not long after you started to walk, you worked out how to open the side gate and go for a walk up the street with your faithful dog Diggity. I was in the house cleaning up, having a glass or two of wine (because I thought I deserved it after doing so much housework), I was not watching you close enough. Thankfully, our little dog would not let you near the road. I found you both after you had made it almost to the corner of our street.

Was my higher power looking after you, while I was being a drunk? I think it must have been, because thankfully nothing terrible happened to you. I know all parents make mistake. Was my drinking something you find unforgiveable? Do you even remember? You were still so young. I would like to know what impact my drinking had on you, but as you will not communicate, I can only imagine that it was not good.

Love always.
Mum

Chapter 8

Jessie had been away working for about eight months. I found it so lonely being a single mother, my days stretched out in front of me. Sticking to a routine in the house helped to keep me busy and not thinking about being separated from my family, who were all still down south. Not being a family with both a mum and a dad for our child was not how I envisioned life to be. I wanted us to be a family again, one that lived together in the one place.

Jessie and I were still in contact; we spoke every day on the phone. It helped a little, but I could not help feeling that he was the head of our family and he should be looking after us properly. He should have been sending money home to help with the bills, instead of me getting the single mother's pension. I had been raised to work and not live on handouts from the government. I was very naïve as to how the world worked.

Jessie's drinking personality was very dominating, and I was becoming a little afraid of him. Even when he was not drunk or hungover, his tongue could be very sharp and hurtful. I would often catch him trying to twist words around to see if I had been lying to him, or if I had been unfaithful to him. He would often belittle me for small things and make nasty comments if he thought I was putting on weight. When his top lip curled, I knew I was in trouble. An argument would start, and it would go on and on, round and round until I was exhausted.

Whenever he came home for a whole week, at first it was absolute joy. The first couple of days we would make love, then talk into the night like two star-crossed lovers. He would bring me gifts, take us out at night, but then as the week wore on, the real-life responsibilities of having a child would start to show. He would get angry because I could not focus all my attention on to him. I organised to have friends over, to distract him and to give me a break as well. We would party through the night, music blaring laughing and drinking. Jessie would order me to bed when I could no longer walk and was too drunk to even crawl. I would be escorted into our room and ordered to go to bed. I would do as I was told, but when I hit the waterbed it would start rocking, the water slurping under me. I would somehow manage to crawl out of bed and through the swinging doors into the sunroom, making it to the window just in time to throw up.

Ruby found me vomiting one night, I was leaning out of the window, and Diggity was lapping it up. I was completely naked. My friend wrapped a blanket around me and pulled my hair away from my face, and when I had finished throwing up she helped me back to bed when my retching had subsided.

As time went on, I found it harder and harder to cope with Jessie coming and going out of our lives. My stress levels were beginning to rise, and I was suffering more dizzy spells. The first time Jessie saw me have one of my turns, his nastiness instantly dissolved into worry. He backed off his harsh words for the rest of the week.

My sister Lynda was preparing for her debutante ball and we decided I would go home to Murray to attend the event. I caught the bus, it was such a long way with a toddler, but I was discovering I had one of those kids who was much like me. She loved travelling and adapted to what every was happening at the time with little to no fuss. In the years that followed we made the trip many times, and there was always a kind lady who would take the child while I made up a bottle or helped to change a nappy. I have always found people who travelled to be truly kind.

Grace lent me a dress to wear to the ball. I organised for Jessie's sister Leigh to babysit for the night so that I could surprise my sister at her ball. I was feeling very deflated from the mental abuse that I had been suffering from Jessie, as well as being a mum who did everything. I got dressed and went to the hall, hiding behind Dad while my sister was being presented. As she and her deb partner came forward, I stepped out from behind our father, smiling when I saw how beautiful my sister looked. She beamed with excitement at seeing me.

That night I was conscious of Dad being in the same room as me. I did not want to drink in front of him. I waited for the main part of the evening to come to an end, when he left to go back to Gran's. As soon as I was sure he was not coming back I cracked my first beer and proceed to make a mess of myself. I do not know how I did not rip Grace's dress as when I woke up in the morning my stockings were torn to shreds and I had lost a shoe. I had very little memory of the night.

I knew deep down inside there was something terribly wrong with the way I drank. I had no control. This was not a new revelation; I had known I had a problem since I was eighteen. I think I had secretly known it from the first time I picked up a drink. I had tried so hard to be just a social drinker, it was important, I felt, to fit in, I was scared if I did not drink when Jessie was home and with my friends then I would lose them. I was facing an uphill battle between convincing myself to stop drinking while on a steep decent to rock bottom, all at the tender age of twenty.

My mother could see my battle and could sense my sadness, I was so very tired when the time was approaching for me to catch the bus home, she worried about me going back. She knew my relationship with Jessie was not healthy. I even heard her talking to Dad on the phone about me; I knew that she must have been worried if she was talking to him.

I called Jessie and told him that we had to end our relationship. He got in the car and drove for eight hours from Cotton to tell me how sorry he was and that he did not want me to leave. He told me all the things I wanted to hear, he even agreed to us moving from Karinga to Cotton so that we could be a proper family again.

I returned to Karinga a few days later, my faith restored in the man I loved.

Despite Jessie's reassurance, the move to Cotton did not happen as quickly as I expected. He made excuses as to why I could not move yet; the winter was setting in, then he wanted to spend his twenty-fifth birthday in Brisbane. We decided to host a cocktail party, something from A to Z. We stocked up on everything we could find and asked our friends to bring a bottle or two to add to the bar. The night was going well until I got to M for martini, the most terrible drink ever invented. For some reason, Jessie was not drinking as much as the rest of us. He would not give me another drink until I had finished that one. I developed a love of olives that night.

Later that week after Jessie had returned to Cotton, Jim, an old friend from Murray came to visit. One night Jim and I decided to go to the movies. The couple who shared our house at the time agreed to babysit while I was out. I thought I was safe. I did not want to drink, I made up my mind that we would go into the city, watch a movie, then come home again. After all, there was more than a thousand dollars' worth of alcohol in our house, I did not need to get it from anywhere else.

I was doing so well until we decided to stop to get something to eat. Jim suggested a bottle of wine between us and I thought that would not be a problem. In the blink of an eye one bottle became two. I do not know why, maybe it was my spirit guides telling me to listen, but on the way home from the movie, one Mongolian lamb and two bottles of white wine later, I remember telling the taxi driver how to get to our house. The driver snapped at me, saying he knew exactly where I lived, that he had been there numerous times to either pick us up for a night out, or to drop us off afterwards, as drunk as lords. For some reason it shocked me, it made me feel uncertain. Karinga was not a small town; for him to remember us, and our house, was unsettling.

We must have arrived home, but I do not remember anything until late the next day. I was shocked at the time and worried that I had not attended to my child in all that time. Alanna reassured me that my baby was okay, but it did not make me feel better. She told me Jessie had been calling since the night before. I had a terrible feeling at the pit of my stomach. I worked up the courage to call him back. It was a phone call that changed my life.

❖

Jessie gave me a choice between my family and drinking. He suggested I should only drink when he came home, but he and I both knew that was not possible, I had already tried so many things to limit my intake, it was all or nothing. This was the light bulb moment, I needed to finally stop, to prevent my addiction to alcohol from ruining my life. I did not want to lose my family, so I stopped, cold turkey. My baby was only seventeen months old. We had a whole lifetime ahead of us, I could not lose those years.

That night was Jim's last with us. We decided to go out to dinner in the city. Sitting in the open air, my hand was shaking as I fed my child. Jim put his hand over mine, took the spoon from me and asked me if I wanted a drink. I declined respectfully. My whole body was shaking from the effort of not picking up a drink. We went home and I went to bed. Sleep was my salvation that first night, and on many more nights as I struggled to stay sober.

I awoke the next morning proud of the fact that I had survived my first day and night without a drink. I said goodbye to Jim and gave him some photos of the baby to drop off to Mum. The house was eerily silent when he left. I lay down on the couch and watched TV for the rest of the afternoon. I decided I would only get up when I was needed.

Mother's Day

Over the following weeks I seemed to be walking around in a haze, trying to cope with not having a drink, working out ways to distract myself. Each morning I got up and did my household chores, then took the baby out for the day to help distract us both. Back at home, I opened the front door and walked into our kitchen where I was faced with rows of coloured bottles. I never moved them, I just left them there as a test of my willpower.

Dad arrived one afternoon not long after I had stopped drinking. This was my spirit world again, talking to others who knew how to help me. He stood at the front door looking at me as I cried for help, trusting him to help me do what I needed to do. As usual, he took it all in his calm and understanding way. He helped me find an AA meeting to go to that day, he came with me and held my hand. It was a terrifying experience and a hope-filled one at the same time. Dad told me to listen to the stories. I felt like a little kid sitting there next to him in a room with others who seemed to be so much older than me.

I was so lucky to have my parents, I could rely on them to listen when I needed help. But when Jessie found out I went to an AA meeting he was angry. He did not think I needed to go to meetings, raging at me that I should stay home with our baby, that I would be okay. I did as he told me.

I white knuckled it through every day, kept my routine, making myself even busier, staying longer at the shops so that I did not have to look at the bottles of alcohol sitting on the shelves. I started to keep a diary, writing in it every time I felt like a needed a drink.

Night-time was the hardest part of the day, not having any distractions, without having someone to talk to. I started to suffer with insomnia, which made it difficult to get up in the morning; it often felt like I had only just gone to sleep.

When Jessie came home, he continued to drink in front of me. I found the smell terrible, and the temptation extremely high. Amanda brought me some non-alcoholic wine so that I could drink without feeling like I was being left out. It helped at the start, but it was not a long-term solution.

I turned all my attention to being an amazing mother. My baby needed me, but more than ever, I needed to be with Jessie. Being new to sobriety was difficult and I was tired of being separated from him. I reminded him of his promise for us to move to Cotton, that I needed to be with him to feel safe. He finally relented and agreed to us moving. It was such a relief to think we would finally be a family again.

I was about to learn that I was stronger than I ever thought. I was only three months sober.

My Darling Charlie,

I know why I always got it wrong; it was because I did not always listen to those around me that were watching me waste my life. I have only really listened when I have been forced, like now. when you will not answer my calls.

I have had to take my painted ears off and put on my listening ears a few times in my life. When It happens, it is so loud that my head feels like it going to cave in. I know then that I need to keep listening, for the sake of my mental health and personal growth.

On that very last day when I was on my knees, at the end of my drinking rope, there was no choice but to stop drinking. It was one of the hardest days I have ever experienced. I had to decide between the two things that I loved most, you, and alcohol. I have never regretted my decision to begin my life again as a sober woman. I could not imagine my life without you in it. There was nothing I would not do to keep us together.

When I started my journey on the road to recovery, I knew that it was not just for me or for you, but for my family as well. Jessie continued to drink and had no plans to give up, so I had to learn how to be around alcohol if I wanted to continue being his partner. I also had to learn how to be around other people when they were drinking if I wanted to continue be the social butterfly that I loved being.

On my own in Karinga, juggling sobriety, motherhood, separation – and, for the first time in a long time, all my emotions – was hard, but I was determined to succeed.

ELIZA JANE

Once again, I looked at how my parents had handled my dad's recovery and I figured that if they could do it, so could I. Except I did not know the full story; the pressure they were both under, other factors in their lives that did not figure in ours. I had to learn how to live life on my terms, not those of my parents.

In the same way, you have learned that you do not have to live your life the same way your dad and I did. You are handling your life in a better, more organised way by the look of things.

Or is it just a front that you are putting up, so that you look like you are doing better than you want us to know? I hope you do not face the same demons I faced. I would not wish that on anyone, let alone my own child. One thing you can be sure of, if you ever need a mother's support, please know I am ready to help you, unconditionally and without judgment.

Love always.
Mum

Chapter 9

Jessie organised for us to catch the bus to Cotton and had booked a room at the pub, as up until then he had been living with his dad in a caravan on the farm My first job would be to find a house for us to live in, but as we would be arriving late in the afternoon after a ten-hour bus ride, we were going to need short-term accommodation. Towards the end of our trip, I could tell we were close to our destination when I saw what seemed to be endless white fluffy fields, full of the plants that gave the town its name.

We settled in for the night, having tea at the pub with Henry, who had come into town to see his grandchild. Henry was a gentle man and very old-fashioned, he believed in treating a woman well. He made me feel welcome and played with the baby. We stayed downstairs for a while until the dining room closed, then I took the baby upstairs while Jessie and his dad headed to the bar. It was hard being inside a pub, I was happy to escape upstairs and get away stench of the stale beer that seemed to seep into my skin.

The next day was forecast to reach at least thirty degrees. We went to one of the local cafés for breakfast, and from the window I could see several real estate offices along the street. I asked Jessie to come with us to look at rental properties, but he refused. I asked him to look after our toddler while I went out into the heat, and once again he refused, telling me I was to take the baby with me while he stayed in the cool of the pub. With no other option, I was forced to take my fair-headed child into the heat. My anger was mounting at how selfish he was being.

I headed out into the already rising dry heat, toddler strapped into the pusher, determined that I would not let Jessie's lack of concern for our wellbeing put me off. I strolled up to the first real estate office and made my inquiry. I looked through the list I was given and chose a few properties that appealed, as well as some that did not, just in case they were more perfect than they appeared on paper. I was given the address of the houses I had selected, asking if they were within walking distance. Most were, fortunately, and with a map of the town in hand I thanked the lady before heading to the other two real estate offices.

After compiling my list from all three agencies I had quite a long list. I realised, looking at the map, that the town was bigger than I imagined and many of the places were not within easy walking distance.

I found the taxi rank and asked one of the drivers for directions, After I explained my situation – Jessie had not given me very much money – and the driver said he would take me for a flat fee of twenty dollars. I think he felt sorry for me, a new woman in town with a baby, and a partner who was too lazy to come out in the heat. It took the driver an hour and half to show me all the houses on my list. Being a local, he knew most of the houses and let me know if he thought they were suitable for us or not. By the end of the trip, I had found us a beautiful house with four bedrooms, which would also accommodate Jessie's cousin Joey who was

Mother's Day

coming to Cotton to work with Jessie and Henry. The house had an ensuite and a dishwasher, a garden full of fruit trees and plants, and high fences.

We secured the house and I travelled back to Karinga to pack up and say goodbye to our friends there. I was sad to leave them but excited for the next chapter in our lives.

We were moving at a busy time. After packing up the house and making sure that everything was on the truck, we travelled by bus to Bloom for the weekend to celebrate Dad's fortieth birthday. We then got back on the bus and headed up to Cotton to start our new adventure. All up we spent two days travelling, crossing two state borders, passing by Cotton on the way south. It was hard going, but I loved the excitement of knowing that after the final stop I would be sleeping next to Jessie again every night.

I arrived in Cotton, exhausted from travelling with a baby, only to find that Jessie had not set up the house, he had left it for me to do. I rolled up my sleeves and got organised. Jessie and Joey helped to get the furniture into the house but then went to the pub for the rest of the day. By the time they got home I had completely unpacked and cleaned up and dinner was on the table. Joey was impressed with my efforts; Jessie did not seem to care; he took it for granted and expected that it was my job to do everything.

We settled in quickly. Cotton is a pretty little place, with lots of gum trees. I would often see koalas in the lower branches across the road from where we lived. I was teaching my growing child about numbers and letters, and we would count the koalas we could see up in the trees.

In keeping with our new life, I was determined to get us into a good routine. I weaned my toddler off bottles, saying

I had left them behind at the old house. As usual there was no real fuss, just an understanding that was how it was going to be. I walked down to the street to do the shopping, the toddler would be in the pram or walking behind me. We quickly made friends with the taxi drivers, who drove us home if I had too much shopping.

Jessie often stayed out late after work and would eventually be brought to the door, completely out of it by one of the taxi drivers. They would ask if I would like a hand getting him inside. "No", I would say, and would manage to get him inside all by myself.

If he did come home of his own accord it would be ranting about the fact that he wanted a freshly cooked meal, not the dried-up one that had been cooked much earlier in the evening and was now in the warming oven waiting for him. He would pick at small things and told me I was lazy, even though our house was showcase cleaned every day. I also washed the curtains monthly and cleaned the windows every other week.

Jessie's nit picking about every little thing I did and how I did it, together with his drunken chauvinistic rants, were beginning to wear me down. I could feel my self-confidence eroding. Self-doubt crept in, and my ability to keep positive and sober were quickly fading. In Karinga I had my circle of friends to help counteract Jessie's bad behaviour, but now I was in a new town, hundreds of kilometres from everyone I knew.

❖

I was not ready to quit yet. I still loved Jessie with all my heart, and I was determined to make a go of it. I did not want to become a single mother and was not ready to give up my dream of a happy family. Deep down inside I knew I was on the verge of a relapse, I needed something to divert my attention. I decided to meet some new people and make some friends; it was also time for my child to start interacting with other children.

I walked past the local childcare centre every day and often wondered about if it was a good idea for my child to go there. I was at a turning point; I knew I needed to find something for both of us, so I built up the courage and I went in to find out the prices. I went home armed with answers to all the arguments I expected to get. When I asked Jessie if he thought it was a good idea to put our child into day care twice a week, to my surprise, he agreed, and he thought it would be good for me as well. Every now and then he acted like a reasonable man; this was the old Jessie that I had fallen in love with, and it gave me hope that we going to be okay.

I was signing all the paperwork on the first day when I noticed a poster for a charity car ride. A woman, bold as you please, basically ordered me to go on the ride with her in her car. I did not know how to take her; she was so bold and brash compared to my meek and mild ways. To this day Sarah still makes fun of the mousey me that I was back then, and of the way I quietly said I'd better ask my partner first. Sarah became my first friend in Cotton, and our children were similar ages. I was starting to feel like I fit in somewhere.

Sarah helped me to get my learner's permit and was gracious enough to give me driving lessons. Every Tuesday after we had dropped the kids off at day care we would go out in her car. My first driving incident involved the KFC speaker box. I did not hit it but was close. I was banned from driving in town for a while. Luckily, there was so much space outside town that I could continue my lessons without worrying about running into something. I really loved these days. We would stop at the café after our driving lesson to have a toasted sandwich before picking up the kids from day care.

Jessie brought me a mountain bike to help me get around town more quickly. It was easy going into town because it was downhill, but I would still often get a taxi home, or one of the taxi drivers would bring it back for me later if I was tired.

My days were spent cleaning, doing all the yard work, making sure that everything was perfect for when Jessie came home. Going to the day care and having my driving lessons gave me things to look forward to, and the days passed quickly.

I turned twenty-one not long after we moved. Amanda came down to help celebrate. There were just the four of us, Jessie, Joey, Amanda, and myself, and it was my first sober birthday. Going up to the pub tested my resolution, but I did not complain because we did not go out very often.

While the others were drinking their beers I drank non-alcoholic wine, but even that was not good enough for Jessie. Every new taunt cut deeper into my soul, but it was true that my dependency on the non-alcoholic wine was growing. I was drinking at least four bottles a day.

I was starting to experience dizzy spells again; they were becoming more frequent, and I was getting worried. I went down the street every day to replace my stash of non-alcoholic wine. One day my body gave out, Jessie came home to find me shaking uncontrollably on the bottom of the shower. He picked me up, wrapped a towel around me and told me I was not to drink any more non-alcoholic wine, it was not good for me. I felt like I was back at square one, I had to learn all over again how to live my life without my addiction. Non-alcoholic wine, I discovered was as hard to stop as actual alcohol. The uncontrollable shakes and the fog that had swirled around me when I had first stopped drinking returned, but not as badly as the first time. This made me realise that the next step would have been buying bottles of real wine again.

As Christmas approached Jessie brought home a real tree. It was so much nicer than the cactus we had the previous year. We celebrated early as I was going home to Murray for Christmas. Joey offered to take us as he was going home to see his family, so I would only need to get the bus back home in the new year. Jessie did not want to go, and he was worried that if I went home, I would break up with him again. I promised him I would not do that, we had been getting along better, and I did not want to uproot myself and my child. When I got home to Murray, I wrote a letter to him telling him how much I loved him and how I never wanted to leave him.

❖

I was happy to be home, to see my family again. Christmas is always a busy time of the year, fitting in all the family members that were spread out between Murray and Bloom. This meant, though, that I had more freedom, with ample babysitters willing to give me a break, I could let down my hair and breathe a little.

On Christmas Eve I wrapped all the presents and, with my small child safe in bed, I headed into town. It was a Murray tradition, every year we would meet at the pub and catch up with old friends to update everyone as to what was happening in their lives. I walked through the main door to be greeted warmly by several people I knew. I stopped and chatted on the way to the bar to get a drink. My heart was racing, I was worried that I would fall back into old habits and ruin all the good work I had done over the past six months in recovery. As I moved through the crowd, I spotted some of the friends I had gone to school with, and friends I once went out drinking with. Each of them took it in turns to hug me and to ask how I was doing. I stood next to the bar to be served.

The boys – Billy, Cam, Josh and Matty – all wanted to buy me a Christmas drink, whatever I wanted. I said I would have a Coke. Cam looked at me and asked if I had given up drinking. I said "Yes!" All four laughed said it was a miracle, and that their wallets would stay fat because I would not drink them dry. I was relieved that they were not going to force me to have a drink or to make me feel ashamed about my decision. I stuck close to them through the night to help give me strength.

I had reached the second milestone in my recovery and succeeded. Waking up on Christmas morning without a hangover, with no guilt or shame, was an amazing feeling. It gave me more confidence. We stayed for two weeks and I had a great time.

Mother's Day

When I arrived back in Cotton, Jessie presented me with an official engagement ring; my letter of undying love must have hit a chord. I was so excited. Everything was looking up. My days seemed brighter again.

Life went back to normal. I joined the day care committee and became more involved with what was happening at the centre. Jessie was still working long hours out on the farm, and he was still drinking, but his sharp tongue seemed to be having a rest. I was enjoying being a stay-at-home mother, doing all my chores and looking after my family.

The tranquillity was short lived. It was like living with Dr Jekyll and Mr Hyde with Jessie. I never knew when his mood would change, and it changed quickly.

His sharp tongue often led to me having dizzy spells. These are caused by high stress, I later I found out they are a form of headache. I had experienced the first one when I was sixteen, my mother had been yelling at me about something when I collapsed. The next one was when I was about seven months' pregnant, and we were living at the boarding house. Having them come now was scary, especially when one occurred while I was riding the bike with my child along the main street. Luckily, I acted fast, getting us both safely off the bike while I waited for the sensation to pass. This usually took about fifteen minutes, but in those fifteen minutes I had to close my eyes because the light hurt them, my temperature rose quickly, and I felt vomit rising into my throat.

❖

ELIZA JANE

Dad came up for my twenty second birthday. It was so nice to have his presence in the house, I could feel his strength and protection. Jessie had ordered two kegs of beer to celebrate my birthday, even though he knew I would not be joining him in sampling the barrel. He started to make his way through the kegs the day before my birthday. With the help of his new farmhand, he drank through the night, and when Dad and I got up the next morning Jessie was totally inebriated and thought he could challenge Dad to a wrestling match. Drunk Jessie was no match for a sober Pat. As much as Jessie tried to take him down, Dad kept getting the better of him. Jessie went to bed humiliated by the fact that he had been beaten by an older man.

As Dad was leaving to go home, he told me that if I chose to leave Jessie, my child would grow up to understand the reasons. I hugged him tightly, not wanting him to leave but understanding what he was saying to me. I knew he was right. I had often thought about his and Mum's marriage ending after he found sobriety, and I couldn't help wondering whether my relationship with Jessie was going the same way.

I was not ready to leave yet. I was not ready to give up on my dream of having a family. Staying became more difficult, however, as Jessie started to become more relentless in his negativity towards me. He would often berate me for not having a job and failing to contribute to the family income.

I did not want to be a burden, so I looked for a job. I had a little bit of experience, but I had no references. After I dropped my child off at day care I went to all the cafes and to the pub to ask if there were any jobs available. I was offered a job in a café, but it did not last long, there was a lot of cattiness and I was too fragile, and the boss saw that. I was then offered a job behind the bar in the pub where we had stayed when I first came to Cotton. Sarah was happy to help with babysitting if I had a shift through the day. I started work and felt like I had overcome an issue that was threatening our relationship, but Jessie was still not happy. He didn't like me working at night and did not like staying home to babysit. He did not like that I was getting a lift home with our neighbour who worked at the bar as well, accusing accused me of wanting to have an affair with him, and with anyone else I worked with. It was too much for my boss to deal with and I was asked to leave. I was disappointed, as being a non-drinker, I enjoyed serving the customers and interacting with the public.

Jessie's drinking was escalating and so was his mental abuse, I never knew what to expect when he came home. I was crying most days; I was at the end of my tether. I had been in recovery for nearly seventeen months and his drinking was putting a wedge between us. It is hard to watch someone else destroying their life and trying to take you down with them. It had become so very toxic that I was beginning to wish that Jessie would not come home at all, so I could just live in peace.

❖

One day I was up early after Jessie had left to go to work. I was awake but stayed in bed until he left, pretending to be asleep. I was doing everything I could do to avoid his rage.

I put on the washing because it was meant to be raining later in the day and I wanted it to dry before the rain came, I fed my child, vacuumed, washed the floors, made the beds, emptied the dishwasher, and packed away the dishes. I stacked the breakfast dishes into the now empty dishwasher, then went down into town to do the day care drop. I was then free to go and pick up the presents that I had on layby for my little one's third birthday. I went home, put the gifts onto the table and started to wrap them so that I could put them away until they were needed three days later.

I heard Jessie come through the door. He strode into the house, I do not think he came home for any particular reason, except maybe to see if I was still in bed. I saw him glancing at the wrapping paper that was on the floor, he looked me in the eye and calmly told me if I did not clean up the house to his standard then I could ring my father to come and get me. With that he turned around and left again.

I sank down onto the kitchen chair. I cried into my hands. I got up to get a tissue to wipe my tears away before picking up the phone and calling Dad. I told him I'd had enough, and I was ready to come home. I was broken.

Dad paid for our bus tickets; we were leaving the next day. I went outside and took the washing off the line, called Sarah to ask if she could please take me up to the laundromat so I could make sure all Jessie's clothes were dry before I left. I took one hundred dollars out of Jessie's account using the broken card he gave me that was held together with sticky tape. I went to the day care centre and told them we were leaving, that I was sorry, but we would not be coming back.

I went home and packed four tea chests with my things. Jessie then went through the chests to make sure I was not taking anything of his, informing me I was not to take any furniture, even the child's. I was not even allowed to take the toy box that I bought as a first birthday present.

Mother's Day

I went to Sarah's place to wait for the bus. I ironed and folded Jessie's clothes and asked her to drop them back around to him for me. She thought I was mad but said she would do as I asked. I got on the bus, hugged my child close to me and cried silent tears as we were taken away from her dad and my love into the new and scary real-life world where we would be on our own again.

ELIZA JANE

My Darling Charlie,

I still feel torn about the decision I made to leave your father. I would have stayed if I could, but the raging alcoholic verbal abuse that I received nearly every day had just become unbearable. Finally, something snapped inside me, and I had to walk away, even if it caused a large festering wound on my heart that never really healed. The last thing I wanted was to break up the family that I so desperately craved, for you and for me.

It was important to me to provide you with the best role model I could. I did not want you growing up with a weak mother, a broken woman who would eventually pick up a drink again if we stayed. I had to choose; to save my sobriety and to save you from a life of watching both your parents descending into the fog of alcoholism, our relationship most probably ending in violence.

I hope you are not resentful that I took you away and broke up our family. I never wanted to disappoint you. I always wanted you to know that all the decisions I made for us - the big life ones - were out of the love that I have for you.

When I left, I made sure I did not take anything other than what was mine. I should have taken more money from the account to help support us, but I never wanted him to be able to say I had stripped him of everything. I had too much pride and dignity.

My own parents' ugly separation and divorce had shown me how not to break up, I was not going to put you through the same anger and hate that I had witnessed as a child.

My parents supported my decision to leave, they could see my sadness, and knew how hard it was for me coming to terms with my sobriety. But they also knew where Jessie's drinking would eventually lead. Your grandfather told me that you would one day forgive my decision to leave, just as I had forgiven him for leaving his marriage to my mum. It was these words of wisdom and support that helped to give me the strength to finally end the relationship. Although, even after I left, I never gave up hope that one day Jessie may change his mind, become sober and realise that I was really the one for him, and that we would be a family again.

I got on with life after Jessie, but it was all a pretence. I may have become sober, but I had not fixed the void. Still with romantic ideas, I filled it with the wrong love, a superficial love. I still hadn't learnt the lesson, that only once I found love for myself and faith in my own strength would I be able to start to fill that void. In the meantime, I had you, and that was the best kind of love. I should have been content with that.

Love always.
Mum

ELIZA JANE

Chapter 10

I sat up straight and wiped the tears from my eyes as Cotton became smaller and eventually disappeared from the horizon. Then, after settling my child onto the seat next to me, I wrapped a blanket over us as we travelled into the night. Having a chance at last to go over the events of the past two days, I leaned my head against the window and wondered how I was going to survive on my own.

In Bloom, we were warmly welcomed. Penny had set up the front room for us to sleep in until I could get back on my feet. She took me to the local Social Security office so I could arrange to get the single mothers pension again. They asked for Jessie's details, I told them that they he would not pay child support, he had never been forthcoming with financial support for our child. I had to wait three weeks for my first payment. I again regretted only taking out a small amount of money before I left, but my pride would not let me take money from his account without his consent.

I found out that I could get a Housing Commission rental bond which meant I could start looking for place of my own. It was great being at home with my family, but it was cramped and as I was now the responsible parent I had to learn to look after myself and my child. With Penny's assistance I found a little unit not far from their house, it was

Mother's Day

also a short walk to the beach. My unit was at the end of the row and we had the place to ourselves for most of the time as the others were holiday units.

Penny and Dad were happy to help out financially to get us set up in the unit, but I was to pay them back. Thanks to my thrifty shopping habits, we found everything we needed for less than five hundred dollars. We moved in and settled down to a new life in Bloom.

I stayed awake for many nights wondering how I was going to manage on a single parent's pension. It was the first time in my life that I would be paying all the bills and buying the shopping using only my money. I had gone from living with Mum, who paid for everything, to living with Jessie who paid the bills and gave me shopping money. I had taken it all for granted, because I was just a kid playing at being an adult. I had so much to learn, but I was determined to do my best.

Our little two-bedroom unit with its small courtyard was big enough for us. I had the phone connected so we could call Jessie and let him know where we were living just in case he wanted us to be a family again. I wished he would change his mind, but he had already moved in with a barmaid from the pub. It had only taken him six days to wipe me from his life. I was completely heartbroken.

I spent most of days at Dad and Penny's where our children could play and have swimming lessons together. My half-brother Tom was only seven.

Once again, I got into a routine to help the days flow easier and to keep me busy. On shopping days, I would walk along the foreshore to the supermarket, collecting shells along the way. (Shell collection was halted for a little while when I came into the kitchen to find some of them on the move along the bench; still with creatures living in them. They were taken back to the beach to live out their lives.)

I spoke to Penny about getting some driving lesson so that I could get my licence. Penny was happy to babysit for me. I paid for professional lessons to help build my confidence. It was scary driving in the suburbs, there were more cars and trucks on the road, and traffic lights to get used to, and many more distractions.

It took me two attempts to get my licence. My confidence was starting to grow again, although my insomnia had returned, I was having difficulty getting to sleep at night. I would lie for hours thinking about Jessie, still hopeful he would come back. It was all wishful thinking; I really did not like being on my own. I felt empty and still thought I needed a man in my life to be complete.

An opportunity to fill that void presented itself one night. My cousins Andy and Bluey shared a house not far from us and I loved hanging out with them. We had grown up together and had many years of fun as kids. Moving back to Bloom was a step that I had not anticipated in my story, but I was making the most of it, and having those two around was always entertaining. While hanging out at Pat and Penny's was good, I was able to relax more and just be myself with the boys.

Bluey decided to introduce me to his mate Dusty. It had only been six weeks since I left Jessie and I did not feel ready to meet anyone new just yet, but I was feeling raw with the news that Jessie had already moved on. Anyway, I have always loved meeting new people.

Dusty looked like a typical surfer, with windswept sun-bleached hair and tanned skin. He was shy when we first met.

There was a boyish charm about him that appealed to me. When he asked me to go to the drive-in with him the following Friday night, I agreed, thinking there was no harm in going on one date.

Dusty picked me up as arranged, he brought his dog along as well. Not a very romantic first date, but I agreed to go out with him a second time. It turned into a whirlwind romance; we could not get enough of each other. It all moved far too quickly.

Dusty lived in the house in Malus that we had once lived in. I thought it was a sign, I had loved living there, I had so many good memories of the place and hoped to make more. So, when Dusty asked me to move in I jumped at the opportunity. Dad was watching carefully; he was not overly happy about me going out with Dusty and now I was taking an even bigger step. I reassured him that I would be okay. He placed his bear size hands on my head and I could see the worry forming in his eyes, but I did not want to believe I had made another mistake.

Now that I had my licence, I could drive Dusty's car when I needed to go to the shops. I was living the life of a housewife again and I was in heaven. Dusty was a member of the local football club and we went to the presentation night together. It was nice to get dressed up and go out, I felt like a princess.

After we had returned home, I was in the bedroom changing when I heard loud banging and shouting at the back door. By the time I got to the door, unbeknown to me Dusty had disappeared out the front door and into the orchard to hide. By this time, the strangers were kicking in the back door. I moved back against the wall as they launched themselves into the house, yelling for Dusty. When I said he was not there, they kicked in the front of the stove while shouting at me that they planned to kill Dusty. After they were convinced Dusty was not inside, they left in search of him. Shaking with fright, I called the police.

I was not aware that Dusty had been fighting with the neighbours for a while, they had finally had enough of him and his antics. The police officer was concerned when he heard Dusty had run off, leaving me to defend myself against three angry men. I thought it cowardly as well, but still I stayed.

Dusty asked me to marry him when we found out I was pregnant. I was looking forward to having my second child, but after that night I had started to watch Dusty more closely. His moods were beginning to swing, and my stress levels were rising again. I was also losing too much weight for a pregnant woman.

I made an appointment with the GP who had been my childhood doctor. She seemed happy to see me again and checked me over and listened while I told her the story of my life since I had last seen her. When I mentioned Dusty's name she looked at me with surprise. She sat down and asked me if I knew about his mental health issues. I said no, he seemed healthy and happy. She told me that her husband had been treating him for a few years since he had moved to Malus. He was meant to be on medication to help keep it in check. I was taken aback. This explained so much. The doctor also told me that there was a chance that I would lose the baby unless I managed my stress levels and stopped dropping weight.

I confronted Dusty about what I had been told. He admitted that it was true, but insisted he had it under control. I really wanted to believe him. I waited and watched to see what would happen, I had a three-year-old and an unborn child to worry about and did not need more stress.

About a week later Mr Bean and his wife came to visit me, Mr Bean was the owner of the orchard where we lived, he told me that if I had not been living in the house Dusty would have already been asked to leave, but because he had respect for my father and my family he had bitten his tongue. However, Dusty had gone too far now and must leave, I knew the house was a worker's house and that my child and I would not be able to stay there on our own.

Dad came over to say he had talked to an old friend who worked on an orchard just outside Stoney, he could provide Dusty a job and a house on the property. I was grateful to my father for once again coming to my rescue. In the same conversation my father told me that he would not come to my wedding if I went ahead and married Dusty. That rocked me to the core, because I could not imagine getting married without my father there to walk me down the aisle.

When Dusty came home I talked to him about the situation. Dusty was angry at Mr Bean and my father, I defended both. He eventually agreed that it would be for the best and we packed up the house and put all our furniture into storage. Dusty told me to take the car and drive to Murray to my mother's house and he would follow on his motorbike the next day.

❖

I left my childhood home once again to go back to Murray, this time as an adult and a mother. I arrived at Mum's at around nine in the evening, when I went inside, I found her pacing back and forth in the kitchen. When she saw me standing in the doorway she burst into tears, telling me that Dusty had called me filthy names and threatened to have me arrested for stealing his car. I was shocked and dismayed at the turnaround in his attitude within just a few hours. I was done. I removed my engagement ring and put it on the counter. I knew then that I could not go back, not only had he disrespected my father but now he had done the same thing to my mother. That was a line that nobody could cross.

Mum agreed to babysit only if I took a family friend with me to return the car. I left the engagement ring with Bluey and told him I was done and did not want Dusty to come anywhere near me. My friend and I caught the train back to Murray. Later that night I started to miscarry, the doctor was right, my weight had plummeted to forty-eight kilos, I looked like a skeleton. It was a blessing really as I had never wanted to see Dusty again. Now, there was no reason.

Jessie came down from Cotton to take our child for a holiday with him and his new girlfriend. My heart broke when I saw my darling wrapped in Jessie's arms. We had never been apart for more than a night since the birth, I felt really lost knowing I would be without my child, even for a short while.

Moving back to Murray had its pluses and minuses. I still had a lot of friends from school there and my social life grew, which went partway to filling the gap left by alcohol and failed relationships. I had grown up with lots of people around me. I had fond memories of going around to my Gran's on a Friday afternoon with a bag of clothes to do a mini fashion show and to get her advice as to what I should wear that night. Her fashion choices were always spot on. I

Mother's Day

kept up the tradition and went around to Gran's to get ready for nights out with friends.

It wasn't enough though. I had changed and now Murray seemed like a bad fit. I found myself repeating old patterns: my love life became chaotic, I was acting like a young girl again, listening to all the sweet little lies about undying love that were told only to get me into bed. I was bouncing around between boyfriends like a naïve schoolgirl, but part of me could see that now. I knew it was not healthy for me or my child.

One morning I woke up, looked out the window and up and down the street, and noticed a heavy feeling in the pit of my stomach. I stopped and listened to my spirit guides working my sub-conscience, telling me it was time to leave, that I did not belong in Murray, it was not healthy for me to be here again. I was trapped in my old cycle and I knew that I did not want my child to grow up in a town that could not forget what I had done.

I decided to move back to Karinga.

ELIZA JANE

My Darling Charlie,

I look back at the period after I left Cotton and I am ashamed of my behaviour. Now I can see that in the years after leaving your dad I was acting like a hormonal teenager who had never been on a date. I was a desperate pain in the butt who thought that I should be in a relationship, and fought for it, even when I knew it was not right.

I was mad at Jessie for moving on so quickly, I wanted him to see what he was missing out on, or what I thought he was missing out on. I think I was a very lost soul who was struggling to find where I belonged. I could not hide behind alcohol anymore, so I hid behind my overinflated ego and low self-worth, two shortcomings that did not serve me very well.

Now I know that the early years of sobriety during my twenties can be summed up as a period when I thought I was invincible. I was young, daring and thought I could do no wrong, that I lived a charmed life that would never end.

I was wrong. The gossip and rumours that circulated were caused by my behaviour, and deep down I knew that I was playing the victim, I just didn't want to admit it. I see that clearly now.

I may have run away from Murray again, but this time I was doing it to protect you from gossip that was attached to me. I did not want you to grow up with tar that had been brushed on you because of my youthful experiences. I wanted you to grow up without baggage, so you would be free to create your own identity.

I have never regretted taking you back to Karinga; that was one of my best ideas, even though I was taking you so far away from our family support. I needed that move to help me grow up.

Mother's Day

I only wanted the best for you. I only wanted the best for us, and I was willing to do whatever it took to achieve that. You were always the focus of most of my decisions.

I know you do not believe that, but it is true.

Love always.
Mum

Chapter 11

Before I made the final decision to move back to Karinga I called Jessie. I wanted to make sure that he did not have a problem with me moving away from Murray. He could not care less. He said it was easier for him to get to Karinga than it was to get to Murray.

I asked my mother if we could move back in for six weeks to save money for my move. Of course, she was excited, it meant she got to spend quality time with her first-born grandchild before we moved a long way away. I purchased Lynda's car, a little Datsun 180B. I was all set for my next adventure.

When the day of our departure arrived, I had made time to see Gran before I left, promising her I would be okay on my own up in Karinga and that we would come home once a year to visit. We left on pension day, knowing I had the funds to get us where we needed to go. We were waved off by my family, I was leaving for the second time in just a few years. My parents advised me to stop whenever I felt tired and to remember to use landmarks so I would not get lost.

It was an easy road to travel. The only real turnoff I made was when I got to Cotton. Jessie had agreed to take care of our child for six weeks while I looked for a job and accommodation in Karinga.

Mother's Day

I had organised to stay with my friends Haze and Shirley who were very happy to put me up while I got myself settled. As soon as I had crossed the border into Queensland, I felt like I was home again. I settled in quickly, spending time catching up with everyone before looking for a job. I was lucky to have a great network of people already. Jim, who had been with me when I had my last drink was now living in Karinga and I loved hanging out with him and his friends. Erin was living in Karinga with her family, and I reconnected with Ruby, Amanda, and Grace as well. I felt a sense of peace and harmony settling over me.

I knew I need to find employment of some kind to help finance my dreams. The single mother's pension was not enough to live on, let alone to lead the lifestyle I wanted. I had always imagined myself in a sales job, so I scoured the paper and found a position. I went in for an interview and was excited to be offered the job straight away. Owning a car was an advantage as it was a door-to-door sales role. I knew I had to start at the bottom and work my way up, and I had the confidence to think I could do that in a week.

Each morning we attended the warehouse to discuss which areas we would be covering and who we would be going out with. We worked in teams of three and were each given a bag full of promotional items, including coloured t-shirts and toys. It was a competition every day to see who sold the most.

We would head out into the heat to our designated areas and walk around industrial sites selling the knickknacks to anyone who would buy them. It was a tough gig, I had never encountered so many uninterested and rude people. Wearing my uniform, I stopped at a store to buy a packet of cigarettes and was told to get out and not to come back, I tried to explain that I was not there to sell my goods but to buy something and I was still refused service. It rattled me, I am a people pleaser and to have upset someone did not sit well with me. But I shook it off and headed out again the next day.

Some days would be great, I would sell most of my bag, it all depended on how my first sales had gone and the success of the yarns I spun to make them sound attractive. On other days I would be left feeling dejected, returning with a full bag and zero sales.

I soon discovered I was not particularly good at selling things to people, which reflected in my paycheque. It was commission based, so the more you sold the better it was in for your wallet. I even tried my luck selling my goods on a trip out of the city with a couple of other salespeople. We loaded up the Datsun and headed towards the town of Peanut, about one hundred kilometres southwest of Karinga, stopping on the way at other little towns. It was a fun little trip; I was able to see more of the countryside, but it was not profitable. I starting to become disheartened, the job was not turning out to be as exciting as I had thought it would be.

One morning I woke up with a sore ankle from a spider bite. Over the day my ankle swelled to the point that I thought I might need to go to hospital, I saw the doctor and thankfully it was not poisoned, but he prescribed some antibiotics to help heal it. When I developed scabies it was the last straw; I handed in my resignation.

I found a little house for us to live in. I had everything organised just in time for Jessie to bring our child home. Everyone I knew had donated some furniture to make the

Mother's Day

place more homely and comfortable. Life began to become normal again now that I had my darling child back with me.

ELIZA JANE

My Darling Charlie,

Moving us back to Karinga was, I realise now, my way of escaping a situation that I had put myself in. I should have faced up to my own failings, listened to what others were telling me, and changed my ways, but I was running away. I had done this for most of my life, because I thought I could find an easier way, a better way. Really, all I was doing was making it harder for myself.

I do not regret moving back to Karinga. I wanted a better life for you, one that did not involve living in a small town full of gossips looking down on you just because you were my child. They thought I was a bad person, and they thought you would grow up to be bad as well. But besides the running away bit, I really needed to learn to stand on my own two feet, even though at times it left me feeling isolated and vulnerable.

Being a young mother on my own, I worried about our future. I had an idea in my head as to what I thought it should be like, but I spent many sleepless nights worrying about finances and the future when I should have been just concentrating on the now, because we cannot predict the future, it never turns out how we imagine.

I drew strength from being back within my strong and independent circle of friends. I only ever wanted good and healthy people in your life, people who would only show us loyal support, as I showed them.

I have always thrived on the strength of those around me, it has given me strength to get through all the hard times. I would have mishandled our lives a whole lot more if it had not been for the support of family and friends.

Mother's Day

Our move certainly helped me to grow up and to show me again that there was life outside a small country town. It was a decision I did not make lightly, and it took a great deal of effort to make it happen, but I think it was worth it, for both of us.

Love always.
Mum

Chapter 12

I loved staying at home as a full-time mother, although the time was slipping away quickly. Thoughts were turning to education, not only for my child but for me as well. Kinder was starting in the new year so I found one nearby and secured a place.

I had always planned that when my child started school I would start working. Being on a single mothers' pension helped when I needed it, but it was not a lifestyle I wanted permanently. I dreamed of being the parent any child would be proud of. Mum and Dad had instilled a sense of responsibility, we knew we were not to rely on the government for our income, that we needed to work to achieve our dreams.

My friends had done a secretarial course through TAFE and they were all doing well. It seemed easy enough, I dreamed of being employed by a huge corporation where I got to wear nice clothes and would rub shoulders with wealthy bachelors. My dream of being married was as yet unfulfilled, so this seemed like a good stepping stone towards that, too. In my mind it was perfect; I went to the local TAFE and enrolled in the secretarial course for the following year.

The plan was to do the drop off at kinder and catch the train to TAFE. On the days when there was no kinder I

Mother's Day

would use an affordable day care centre close by. I had it all worked out. I relaxed and enjoyed the summer.

ELIZA JANE

My Darling Charlie,

The last year of the century was a busy year for us. You started kinder and I went back to school to learn how to be a secretary. I loved being at collage with the other students. I imagined myself as a supermum, I thought I was managing so well, I could do it all. I was operating at full speed and in high gear.

I should have seen the signs and slowed down, stopped to smell the roses as they say, but I was impatient to start making lots of money and to start having the life we deserved. Over the course of my life, I have begun lots of things with great gusto, only to fizzle before the end.

I started to feel like a failure, especially when I was starting to struggle financially, juggling the costs of my education, childcare, and general costs of living. I quit my course less than half-way through, thinking I had learned enough, but I did not have the piece of paper to say I had graduated.

As we both know, you did not grow up with a mum who worked as secretary. My only job in that field lasted just six weeks; it taught me that working in an office was not for me. This was a shame as it had been so close to home, I saved money on public transport costs by walking to and from work.

I felt deflated when I lost my job, while I had known it was not really what I wanted to do for the rest of my life I did love having the extra money coming in and being out of the house every day.

Unemployment kept me up through the night. I worried more than I ever showed. During the day I maintained my 'can-do' attitude, but often, after you were in bed, I cried myself to sleep.

Mother's Day

As I had predicted, your dad did not provide regular financial support. He only helped if I asked, which was frustrating as I did not want to appear weak, but at the same time I was angry that he did not willingly support his only child.

I sometimes wish he had decided to leave at the first opportunity, when I first found out I was pregnant with you. While I would have still been an alcoholic and may have not given up drinking as early as I did, I think I would have managed our lives differently. Would it have been for the better? I do not know, but I do know it would have been easier on my heart if he had not been around, because I would never have seen the disappointment in your face when he did not show up for a scheduled visit.

I turned twenty-five in the last year of the twentieth century. I imagined that I was now a grown up, and I reset my goals: to find a new job, to get married before I was thirty, and to have another child.

Only one of those goals would be achieved.

Love always.
Mum

Chapter 13

I never imagined that the first day of school would be such an emotional day, so much so that I slept through the pickup. Luckily, my neighbour was collecting her own children and brought my child home.

I did not make that mistake again. After losing my job I had settled back into a housewife routine, the days were turning into weeks and months. On the weekends I would go out with my friends, sometimes I met Jim and his friends at a pub for happy hour on Sunday afternoon.

I started looking for work, applying for jobs that I was not qualified for but thought I could do, only to realise that I was only capable of working in hospitality. I eventually found a part time job in a café in the city and was able to access before or after school care, depending on my hours. Being in an area that serviced office workers, the café was only open during daylight hours and from Monday to Friday, with the bonus that the owner was flexible enough to accommodate a single mother.

I was excited to be back at work.

❖

Mother's Day

Sarah and I kept in contact after I left Cotton; our friendship had not wavered and had grown even stronger. We had regular weekly phone catch ups when we would fill each other in about our lives. One day Sarah called to explain that she had a young friend named Hank who was moving to Karinga and was looking for somewhere to stay. She asked if I had room to take him in, I said that I had a couch he could use, and that I was happy to help.

Two weeks later there was a knock on the door and there stood Hank, ready to move in. He only just fitted into our little pink house! he was a big man, and my two-seater couch was not very comfortable. My neighbour, who had air-con in her bedroom, invited him to stay with her. When it fizzled with the neighbour, we decided to move into a bigger house that would provide more room for us all. It also gave me an opportunity to live in a house that I could not afford on my own.

The only thing that I had asked for when choosing the new house was that it was near the primary school my child was attending, and on the public transport route so I could get to work easily. We found a house in a new estate behind the school, it was in a perfect location and only a short walk from our old pink house. This house had four bedrooms and was in a court that was protected from high traffic, I felt it was a safe place for the neighbourhood kids to come and play. I gave the master bedroom to Hank as I felt it was not fair to make him share a bathroom with a small child.

I was now able to start work earlier in the mornings as the school was within safe walking distance for my preppy. I started to feel like life was becoming settled for the both of us, and my child would have the stable home that I had always wanted.

One Saturday morning I was woken by a knock on the door. I opened it to see an older woman standing there. She introduced herself as Mary, explaining that she lived across the road with her disabled son, Anthony. Mary welcomed me to the court, I was taken back by such a beautiful soul. We became friends, helping each other with the care of our children when needed. Life was good – for a while.

Mother's Day

My Darling Charlie,

I realise now that people should only become a parent once there is a level of stability in their lives. This includes financial stability, but also emotional stability. Being a parent involves a great deal of sacrifice. The wrong reason to have a child is because you know there is something wrong with the way you are drinking, and because you think having a child will help you solve this problem. A child should not be required to grow up along with their parents, the adults in their life should already be grown up.

I was not a grown up, I was just a little kid pretending to be grown up. A little kid playing house with a real-life doll.

Regardless of my age and maturity though, you were always my priority, even if you did not think so. I was building a village around us, only allowing people I trusted with my life to be in our inner circle. Those people are still very close to us to this day.

Charlie, when you think about our village back then, what do you see? I see a group of single people, people who were living their lives without the responsibility of having children to look after. This meant I was living in two worlds at the same time. It was an eternal struggle. I lived from Monday to Friday as your mum, making sure you were happy at school, going to work to provide for us. On the weekend I was Wendy, the carefree party girl, craving freedom. It was such a fine line that I walked, even though I probably gave more time to 'Wendy' than I did to being 'Mum'.

I saw a photo yesterday from the one and only time Sarah, my friend from Cotton, visited us in Karinga. You had been crying, you did not want me to go out and it showed on your sweet little face.

ELIZA JANE

You are holding onto my arm, not wanting to let me go. I remember that night all those years ago and I how I was annoyed at you for trying to stop me from having some fun. I am sorry.

Now I realise I did go out too often, as a parent I could have been a lot more dedicated and attentive to your needs. Do you think if I had stayed home more often it would have made a difference to our relationship?

My Darling Charlie, I have already said this, and I will continue telling you, until you hear me properly. You have always been my driving force in life, and the more Jessie disrespected us as a family, the more I wanted you to see that you had a parent that could do it all. I wanted to be a tower of strength and set a good example for you.

I hoped that as you grow older you will be proud of me for standing tall through all the years, and while I made mistakes, I hope you will come to look past them and appreciate the sacrifices I made to ensure we had the best life in difficult circumstances.

Love always.
Mum

Chapter 14

I loved living in the street near the school. It was a safe place; all the neighbours knew each other, and the kids could play without the worry of cars speeding past. It reminded me of my own childhood, the serenity of the area made me feel that life was as it was meant to be.

I became a mother hen, looking after everyone, Hank was like a big kid and I was teaching him how to be responsible. I paid the rent and all the bills, and he paid me his share.

Our house was always busy with people coming and going. Jessie came to help celebrate our child's sixth birthday. The main present was a bike. I could not watch as my precious child learned to ride so I stayed inside while Jessie provided the training. I did not care to witness the inevitable accident, to see tears or hear screams. (I was waiting for the ambulance siren – I was a bit overprotective then).

Much to my relief, about an hour later Jessie forced me to go outside to see our child happily riding up and down the street without training wheels. My heart filled with a mixture of pride and relief that my worst nightmares had not come true.

Jessie stayed for two weeks, providing a glimpse of stable family life. When he visited, we endeavoured to do things together as a family. Jessie never undermined me as the dominant parent, at least not while I was looking. After he left it felt like we were left behind again, he would not call to talk to our child, but left it to me to call him. I had the feeling that as far as Jessie was concerned it was a case of 'out of sight, out of mind'.

On most weekends I was still going out with the girls to parties or pubs in the city. As we were all single, we were each actively looking for the perfect man to begin a relationship with, one that would lead to the marriage, and for me, more children and the happy ever after life that I deserved. I was not having a lot of luck though. They all seemed to have an excuse, I was told I was too happy, or not quite what they were looking for. As payback, I would use a man for my own pleasure, in the same way that I had been used. I could discard them in the blink of an eye; it made me feel powerful and empty at the same time.

I did not seem to have a stop button when it came to men. It was easy enough to meet them, but not to get them to stay with me for any length of time. I always seemed to meet great guys that I had a connection with, but there would be just one thing that stopped us from getting too close.

Once I met a man who I shared an instant connection with. It was during a home visit to Murray; I was invited to a house-warming party by a friend of Mum's. To support herself later in life Mum had become a truck driver, and that was how she had made friends with Wally, another truck driver, who was closer to my age than hers.

Wally had purchased his first home in the up-and-coming area of Cornerstone. It was not a big house, but he was proud of his achievement. He invited us to his house-warming

Mother's Day

party. I did not know many people, so I was not really enjoying myself, until I noticed a man coming through the front door. My eyes were instantly drawn to his face, he stirred something deep in my soul. Wally introduced this man as his Uncle Fred.

I smiled at Fred and imagined that he would be the one I would talk to through the night. Soon I heard, "Wendy, meet Fred's girlfriend Rochelle". I snapped out of my reverie. Of course, he has a girlfriend, I said to myself.

Wally and I have become very good friends over the years, but I did not encounter Fred again for a least twenty years. Still, as I went back to Karinga, back to my life, Fred's image and that meeting stayed with me.

Dad and Penny had moved up to Queensland and were living in a small country town called Bijou. It was nice to have family only a couple of hours' driving distance away. I was able to visit them regularly, and Penny would help with grandchild care over school holidays if Jessie was unavailable.

Grace asked me to share a house with her. I thought it was a good idea as Hank's girlfriend had moved in with us. The house seemed much smaller with two women with huge personalities in it, especially when we did not see eye to eye.

Penny came in the ute to help me move seven doors up from our old house. All day we carried boxes up the street from one house to the other. The back of the ute was piled up with the heavier furniture, two women doing all the work. All men in my life conveniently disappeared whenever I was moving.

Our new house was more open than the house I had shared with Hank. It had lots of light, and being on the corner there was more room on one side. We made the family room that was attached to the open plan kitchen and dining room our main living area. The front room was left unused.

Grace had the master bedroom with the ensuite, and I shared the other bathroom with my child. It was a comfortable house. Every Friday Grace ordered fish and chips for tea and I picked it up on my way home. If Grace had a cigarette in her hand when I opened the door, I knew there was bourbon in her glass of coke.

Friday nights were spent dancing and socialising at the local tavern. Our group was expanding. Chloe was one of the new girls, she and I had a lot in common. She was also from Victoria, and had worked in the high country. She had also lived in Bunji, where I was born. Monica was the baby of the group, but the most outspoken. My circle of friends seemed complete. We each had characteristics that complimented each other's strengths and weaknesses. We did everything together.

I was still the mother hen, looking after everyone, being the positive force in their lives. I did not let anything get me down, until one night when Penny called to tell me that Dad had collapsed in the bathroom and had been rushed to hospital. He was not yet fifty. I had been sitting at the kitchen table talking to Grace and consoling Chloe who had just lost her grandmother when I got the call. Penny said they thought he had cancer. Both girls looked at me as the tears began to roll down my cheeks. Neither woman was able to speak, it had always me that knew what to say in situations like this.

I hired a car and drove to Bijou. Peter, Nathan, Lynda, and Anna drove through the night to be by Dad's side. Sam had been living with Dad and Penny and was at school with our half-brother Tommy. Just twenty-four hours after we got the news all seven of us were by his side. After we were evicted from the hospital, we all camped at the house, waiting nervously to see what the doctors would say.

To pass the time, Peter and Nathan got to work on the house, enclosing the area underneath the stairs My sisters helped Penny, while I seemed to go into hibernation. I had always thought as being the eldest that I would be the one to step up in adulthood when one of our parents got sick or passed away, but I did not know what to do, I did not want to face the possibility of losing either one of them. Dad is my hero; I could not imagine what life would be like without him in it.

The doctor's original finding was incorrect, Dad's lung had collapsed from years of being a heavy smoker and a coffee drinker. Working as a truck driver, he had been slowly working his body into the ground. He gave up cigarettes that day, he also scaled back the number of long-haul trips he was making to recover his health and fitness.

❖

We all watched from afar as we got back on with our lives. I had started a new job in a restaurant that had been built inside an old Queenslander not long before Dad fell ill. I was learning the operations of a five-star restaurant, setting the tables for a la carte dining in the evenings, and working at the counter serving morning teas and lunches.

Some of the customers were mothers who met regularly after school drop-off. I often listened to their conversations about the school that their children were attending. It seemed so different to the state school my child was attending, where the teachers did not seem to care about kids becoming bored and getting into fights. I began asking questions about the school where the parents were sending their children.

It was a Catholic school called St Rita's, co-educational at the primary level and single sex college for high school. I knew private schools were expensive, so I did not get my hopes up, but I had a meeting with the school secretary who told me the school was flexible with payments. If I could set up a payment plan and stick to it, the school was happy to take my child in the new year.

I thanked her and said I would think about it. As with all big life choices relating to my child, I wanted to discuss the idea with Jessie. I also hoped he might offer to pay for it in lieu of the child support he had never paid.

Jessie was in a new relationship with a woman who was older than me, with children who were older than mine. She seemed to dislike me. I had not met her, but we had talked on the phone. I wondered what Jessie had told her about me. I knew that Barbara, the barmaid he had been seeing had ended the relationship because of Jessie's drinking and his violent treatment of her.

I pushed past my fear and reassured myself that it was a reasonable request. To my surprise, Jessie was happy for our child to change schools and said I always made the right decisions in such matters. I was relieved to be able to provide my child an education that I would have only dreamed of, because Mum and Dad could have never afforded to send all of us to such a place.

The final decision came when I attended the parent-teacher interviews at the state school. The teacher told me that I was unrealistic about my child's intelligence and capabilities. I was simply a mother who had delusions about her child's potential. I knew then that I would be signing up at St Rita's the next day. My kid was going to have the best education I could afford.

ELIZA JANE

My Darling Charlie,

Was my choice of schooling for you the right one? Was I right to uproot you and send you to the Catholic school? Ensuring that you received the best possible education was important to me. I knew I was only going to have one chance at motherhood, and I wanted to be the best mum I could be.

I started you off in state school because that was all I thought I could afford. The school was also close to home, you could walk there and back when I was working, and people were always looking out for you.

I had great faith in the school to begin with, you seemed to be doing so well until you reached grade three when I started to see you becoming a bully, getting into fights with other kids. You also seemed to be bored, I worried that the education they provided was not challenging enough. It worried me, both the change in your behaviour and the fact that you were already becoming quite secretive.

I had already started researching state high schools in our area and was hearing about drugs and gang violence. I did not want you to be lost in a school with more than a thousand kids, I wanted your talents to shine through and I knew a smaller school would provide the right environment for that.

My decision to send you to the private school was to get you the best education, and to have a chance to do things I had dreamed of but never had. I wanted you to be around people who were affluent and hoped you would be provided with good role models having high moral standards. I hoped that they would rub off on me too, or maybe

I would meet a single rich dad. I could only dream! (That was a little joke.)

I was naive in believing that Jessie would have helped financially. I had not asked much of him and when two people have a child, they should share the responsibility equally. In my heart of hearts, I knew I would be paying for your schooling and would not be getting much help from him, but I have never regretted the sacrifices I made, and I am extremely proud of myself for ensuring that your school fees were always paid, in full and on time, by me.

Were my good intentions and sacrifices wasted? Do you resent me for changing your school?

Love always.
Mum

Chapter 15

The new year brought big changes. New uniforms, books, and shoes were required for the new school. We needed new bus timetables and to work out a route map. I was worried beyond belief for the first few weeks of the new school term. Mary still rang if my child had not checked in with her on the way to school.

The new year also saw me enrol in a course in psychology to help me get into University. I still dreamed of helping people to overcome their addictions. I went back to work in the café in the city where I was offered a shift from six am until nine am, then I was off to school until three.

My life was on the up. I was busy, but I was happy, I was carefree, and I was excited about how my life was turning out. I was running on adrenalin. My child was adjusting to the new school and I could already see improvements in all subject areas.

The only thing I could not control was my personal relationships. I seemed to only be attracted to men who did not want to be in a committed relationship but were happy to hang around for some fun. I was their number one girl, they would tell me, while dating other girls and encouraging me to go out and find a new boyfriend. I would accept it for what it was, acting like it did not matter. I told myself I was mature and could handle anything, even when I felt empty on the inside. I was desperate to have someone who would not only hang out with my friends but who also wanted to take that next step and build a life together. The men in my life were elusive and kept me wanting more, I should have walked away when they said they were not ready to commit, rather than throwing myself at their feet begging them not to leave.

My social life was expanding, and I had started dabbling in recreational drugs, just every now and then. I was conscious of my addictive personality and did not want it to become a huge part of my life. I did not think taking drugs was bad, but gradually they started to take over my life. My girlfriends watched from the sidelines, not happy with my life choices, they were very vocal to my deaf ears, but also supportive.

I excused my behaviour as a form of release, it helped me to blend into the crowd. I knew I could not drink, and drugs were harder to get so I thought I was safe. Jessie and I had made a pact when we first became parents that we would not take any form of drugs in front of our child, or at least this was to be concealed. I honoured that agreement and felt as a parent, my child did not need to know everything that was happening in my life.

I started going to concerts and festivals, any excuse to let my hair down. I believed it was my life, my choice. I still had a job, I was still providing and taking good care of my child. But, like any addiction, drugs were slowly eroding my life around the edges. Denial was my defence, even though deep down I could feel myself starting to drown in depression, and the constant craving for drugs was starting to crowd all my waking moments.

My life really started to shift when Grace met her future husband Rocky and moved in with him. The house was just not the same without her there. The idea of sharing with strangers made me feel uneasy, like I needed to be constantly on guard, even though the rental agreement was in my name and I called the shots. I put up notices for a new flatmate at the local shopping centre and waited.

One day not long after Grace had moved, I received a call from a foreign sounding woman asking me if I wanted her husband. It took me a few minutes to understand what she was talking about. I had always prided myself on not sleeping with other women's husbands. She told me that she had had enough of her husband and he needed to move out as they were getting a divorce. I said sure, why not, send him around and we can have a chat. I could not be too picky as I could not afford the rent on my own, my budget had always been tight.

'Richard not Dick' (he did not like being given nicknames) arrived later that afternoon for a meeting. He had a stable job, was much older than me and seemed to have a lot of quirks. Quirks do not usually worry me and can get along with almost anybody. I agreed to take him in because he was reliable for his share of the rent and I thought that even with all our differences life together could not be too hard.

Between paying for private school fees, public transport, and daily living requirements, I was also a smoker and I consumed a lot of Coca Cola. When I went out with my friends, they would usually shout my drinks as payment for driving them home at the end of the night. I was taking from Peter to pay Paul, but still, most of the time I struggled to pay anything back.

My life really started to unravel when I discovered that I could not complete my studies in the psychology course as the place where I was studying turned out to be fake. The dean had been using the campus as a front to take money from overseas students. We found out that not one of the courses was recognised for admission purposes by any university. We all lost our money. It was a blow to my confidence as I really wanted to advance my education and get out of hospitality. I also wanted to fit in better with the other mothers from the private school.

When Jessie announced that he was going to be a father again I was devastated and extremely jealous. I was the one who always wanted to have another child. Why was he able to create another life when he did not even show enough attention to his first? It would be three years before he made contact again.

The tension in my house was growing as Richard's quirky character was clashing with my outgoing personality. He knew when he moved in that I was a smoker, but every time I went out the back for a smoke, he would slam the windows shut in a melodramatic manner. He had the main bathroom to himself and one day I had gone in to check if it needed to be cleaned only to have to back out from a metallic stench that made me reel. Richard did not approve of my friends and made a scene whenever they came to visit. I now knew why his wife had wanted him out. 'Richard who really was a Dick' was well past his use-by date when I told him he had to go.

I stayed in the house and paid the rent on my own, most of the time with great difficulty.

❖

Soon after my thirtieth birthday my brother Sam asked if he could stay with me. Dad and Penny were moving back to Murray, but Sam had met a girl and was in love. Dad wanted him to go home with them as he was not fond of the girl; I took pity on Sam and agreed to have him. I helped him to find a job before the end of the summer so Dad could not force him to go home. I thought I was being a good sister in not making him pay too much rent as he was finding his feet, but the financial strain was growing.

I found an internet site called Couchsurfing. It seemed like a great way of meeting new people and for introducing a foreign culture into my child's life. I searched through the list of people looking for accommodation and found an English girl my age who was looking for somewhere to stay. Vivian and I met for coffee and hit it off instantly, it was like we had met before in a past life. Viv did not eat meat, and she was an exercise junkie, but very relaxed and down to earth. She was the perfect addition to our house. I borrowed a car from Hank and picked her up that afternoon. Together we moved her eight-foot surfboard and backpack into the front lounge where she would be staying.

Viv stayed with us each time she was in Australia. She was a sunseeker who liked to avoid the English winters. A real dynamo, she introduced me to rock climbing and other outdoor activities. A new and upcoming company was offering a deal which meant I could do as much rock climbing, kayaking and other activities as I wanted for less than twenty dollars a week. I loved it all.

I was going rock climbing three to four times a week, kayaking twice a week, and taking regular yoga classes. I lost ten kilos in the first three months. My body was becoming toned and sleek, it stroked my ego as well due to all the extra attention I was receiving from the males in my life. My self-confidence skyrocketed; I was going out on more dates. I thought that now I had a good body and more confidence in myself I would finally find my perfect partner.

My 'high on life' period was destined not to last. The slow descent began when the real estate agency told me that they would not be renewing my lease. The owner wanted it for his family members who were visiting from overseas.

I began to look for another house for us to move into, Sam was non-committal as he was now engaged to his girl and would be moving out after he got married. I felt exhausted and wanted a break from sharing a house with other people. I was also becoming very tired of working in hospitality and was worried about the irregularity. I needed a stable income.

I kept up my happy exterior when I was out of my room, nobody would have known that I was struggling mentally. Inside I felt like I was drowning in the thick fog of depression that was starting to surround me. I never wanted anyone to know that I could not cope, that I was at the risk of hitting rock bottom.

I was able to find a house for us to live in at the last moment before we were to be kicked out. I took it, thinking that I would only stay for a little while until I found something better.

This move took us away from our safe and happy environment in Karinga, and a lot further away from St Rita's. The new suburb did not have the same shine as the little haven that we had lived in for the last six years. Our new neighbours were friendly, but not as friendly as Mary. I did not feel safe in this house, even when it was locked the front door could be opened with a little push. From the start, I hated living there. It had a bad aura.

Moving to this house, I could feel myself being forced into a stereotype that I had fought hard against. I already hated being a single mother, and now I was living in a Housing Commission area – and a poor looking one at that. I felt like I had failed both of us, living in a house that was dark, dingy, and falling apart. There was no privacy; there was a crack in the Besser block wall that was wide enough to let in the weather. The threadbare orange carpets did not look like they had been cleaned in years, and even after I had vacuumed they looked like they needed to be done all over again. Wallpaper was peeling in the small and poorly thought-out bathroom. This house was threatening to get the best of me, I was teetering on the edge of a breakdown, back peddling as quickly as I could to try and stop the darkness descending.

To add to my woes, there was no train station nearby and the buses started too late to get me to work on time. I found myself having to get up at four thirty every morning to walk forty-five minutes to the nearest train station so I would be in time for my six am start. Thankfully, the buses were running by seven, so I did not have to worry about my child walking through the streets in the dark to get to school.

Mother's Day

Getting to work was hard enough, but once I got there it was not much fun either. My patience was being tested. The young couple who had taken over the café were running it into the ground and would not listen to advice from anyone. It was not a happy place.

I was by now doing recreational drugs every weekend. I was burning the candle at both ends between waking up early to get to work, keeping up my sporting activities, juggling motherhood and having parties every weekend. My energy was starting to crash and found myself skipping the exercises to come home and go to sleep.

Thanks to Molly, a former work colleague, I secured a job working with her in a furniture retail shop. I started to feel energised, I thought I would excel at this job, but I soon discovered I was not cut out for retail either. An honest person, I could not get over how blatantly people lie to make a sale. I was good at stretching the truth, but I was not cut out for the cutthroat tactics that were used. That, together with the backstabbing and working for commission again made it a tough industry to make a living in. It reminded me of the first job I had when I came back to Karinga.

I was asked to leave that job after another employee objected to my sense of humour. I knew they were jealous that I was popular with the other staff and customers. I was told to leave on the spot. I was not unhappy about losing my job, but it put me back at square one again. What was I going to do with my life and career? One of the sales ladies thought my dismissal was unfair and suggested I work for her ex-husband in a smaller retail shop.

My new job lasted for about three months, I did not really have the heart for selling furniture, my passion was not ignited, and while I was good on the floor, I was not out on the road, which was where I was most needed. We mutually agreed that I should leave, and I went back to Murray for a holiday in the hope that I could perk myself up. I came back feeling more dejected than when I had left.

I began to fret about not being able to find work and I dreaded going back into hospitality. One day I was talking to a lady at the video store who said she had heard they were looking for people in community aged care. She gave me the phone number and suggested I call, she thought I would really love this work.

I went home and thought about the prospect of going into aged care. I always enjoyed spending time with my grandparents, and I had also looked after Mary's son who had a disability. A career change was just what I needed to help dispel the dark clouds that seemed to be getting thicker around me. I convinced myself that I had what it took to be a care worker and summoned the courage to call the number I had been given.

I was called in for an interview within a few days and the following morning I got the call to say that I had been successful. I was so excited that I had a job as a community support worker, it seemed like the first 'real' job I had ever had. I called Dad to tell him; he said I had finally found a job that suited me.

I found myself working alongside women who were a similar age to me, or slightly older. They were down to earth and willing to help and support me as I learned what was expected of me.

I was given a work car to drive during my shifts, and a mobile phone, meaning I did not have to use my own vehicle

Mother's Day

and phone. I was in a work environment where I received encouragement and support from the management team as well. My team leader Mandy was a single mother and said that if my child was ever sick and I needed to go home, she understood. I finally felt like I finally fitted in somewhere. I loved working with the elderly; the stories they told fascinated me, and they appreciated everything that I did for them. I felt wanted and needed, it made me feel like I had a purpose in life. The hole inside of me began to fill up. This job saved me from falling into the depression that had been forming around me for just a little longer.

ELIZA JANE

My Darling Charlie,

Do you remember moving from our safe and happy neighbourhood to the dark and dingy falling-down-around-our-ears house in that very poor suburb? That move dinted my spirit beyond repair. I was already living with depression, fighting against the dark clouds that were descending on me a rapid pace.

I did not expect the neighbours would be much different to the ones that we had left behind. Naively, I thought things would stay the same, but they didn't. These neighbours thought it was fun to contact the council to report me for not mowing the lawns, or to call the police if my music was too loud.

Living off the government went against everything I had been taught. I hated being a single mother, hated that I could not give you the family with a mum and a dad and the nice house that you deserved, with enough money, nice clothes and holidays that were not just down to Murray to visit the family. I was always fighting, it seemed, against the stigma of being a single mother, a former alcoholic, and even sometimes, just being a strong woman.

I felt that the new suburb was an example of all those stigmas I was fighting against: mothers with multiple children to different dads, living in government houses, reliant on handouts, fighting addictions. They argued that their parents lived well enough, so they could do the same. The thought that I was now living like this left me deflated. Did moving here mean I was going to become one of them?

It makes me seem like a snob, but I do not think I am! I always wanted better for us. I did not want to settle for less than we deserved.

Mother's Day

I thought the effort I was putting into our lives was making you happy. I wanted to be the cool and fun mum, the one who was not like a helicopter hovering around all the time getting in your face, but a mum who was there when you needed someone to talk to. But you were not happy, I see that now. You really wanted me to be the mother who pestered you.

Instead, you obviously felt the need to become the parent in our relationship. You thought you needed to tell me how to behave and what to do. I was never going to let you take on that role, even after my breakdown. I always wanted to be the best mum for you, even if it killed me. Fortunately it didn't, I'm stronger than that, as I can see now that I am a survivor. But I still miss you Charlie, my life only makes sense with you in it. Can you forgive me?

Love always.
Mum

Chapter 16

My thirties were not turning out to be much fun. I was using recreational drugs more frequently and I was seeing a boy who enjoyed dabbling in them too. It was really the only thing we had in common. I was allowing him to use me, but at the same time I was being manipulative to keep him interested. It was another toxic relationship that I did not belong in, but stayed in because I thought I needed to. In my thoughts I imagined that if I stayed skinny, cooked nice meals, and did what he wanted, he would want to stay. I was kidding myself. I should have left when he said to me, "You are everything I am looking for in a woman. But!!!!"

But? I wanted to know what that missing piece was, what was that piece that was always missing? Was I not ladylike? Was I too strong, or too weak? Did I not work hard enough? Did I ask for too much from them?

When the relationship finally came to an end, so did what was left of my mental health. In fact, it came crashing down so fast that it took me by surprise. I could feel myself slipping, I tried to stop it, to distract myself from the darkness that was starting to overtake my brightness. I gave up smoking thinking it would help to take my mind off everything. It only worked for a little while.

Mother's Day

I threw myself into work, taking on every shift I was offered. I went out on the weekends, distracting myself from the pain and anguish inside. Nothing was working.

My weight skyrocketed. It made me feel more tired and lethargic. I would come home from work, cook tea and go to bed. Sometimes I did not make it as far as cooking tea, I would just go to bed and sleep, which seemed to be the only thing that stopped me from thinking and worrying. I knew that I was sleeping more than I should, I did not want to feel like that. I wanted to feel like I used to, I wanted my old energy back. I wanted to get up daily and do all the things I had always done as a mother.

I did manage to get up every day and go to work. If I could pay the bills, keep a roof over our heads and put food on the table I felt like I was staying afloat. With a teenager at private school, though, sometimes my money just did not want to stretch that far. I worried about the future. I could not even manage the present.

Jessie only helped when he felt like it, or if he had a bit of extra cash. Whenever he gave me a little bit of money, he thought he was being generous, it never occurred to him that he was just paying some of what he owed. The pressure was building, I started to feel like I was out of my body, that I was just a shell of the woman I once was. The real me was floating somewhere outside, detached, like it was searching for my spirit so it could re-enter my body, but I was lost, too out of sync to manifest anything worthwhile.

Nobody noticed my decline – if they did, they did not say anything. To them I was probably the same Wendy, always addicted to something or other. It was what they expected of me. There were comments about my weight. I joked them off, put on my positive face and made light of them. I retreated further into my shell where I could not be hurt. Nobody could get close enough to see I was at that point in my life that where I had no defences left. I did not even have the energy to shower. I would take my clothes into the bathroom with all good intentions, only to turn around and go back to bed.

My house was becoming messy, my usual Saturday morning routine was now non-existent. Where once I was meticulous, what I did was sporadic and careless. I was fighting with a hormonal teenager who did not want to do anything to help around the house, while at the same time telling me how ashamed they were at living in what they thought was a pigsty. It was not that I did not want to clean, my values had not changed. I just did not have the energy. I just wanted to lie in bed and cry all the time.

I tried going to a few different doctors to ask for help. Initially they did not seem to know how to help, and I left feeling like a fake, wondering if I was making it all up. Despite their judgment I kept making appointments; I was desperate for a solution.

I was imagining more and more often that it might be easier for my child to go and live with Jessie, then I would be free to end my life. I was useless anyway; I was not the mother I should have been. I had failed not only my child but myself as well.

My wish was coming true. Towards the end of Year 9 my teenager decided to move in with Jessie for the start of the new year. I agreed, reluctantly. It seemed like the only option.

Mother's Day

Jessie was resistant to the move. Later in the year when I travelled to Murray for Mum's fiftieth birthday, I decided to stop off at Jessie's to organise the transfer to the local high school for the following year. This proved to be a more difficult exercise than I expected. Jessie had moved to an even smaller town about two hours' drive from Cotton, he would not give me his address or any information to help with the enrolment. I should have seen the signs; he was determined to cut us off completely.

I went to the office at St Rita's to tell them of the change of plan, that the move would not be happening. While talking to the assistant principal I had a panic attack and broke down in tears. I had built myself up for the move, built up myself for the end, and now there was no end. I was at breaking point.

One of my elderly clients saw that I was struggling and suggested I see her GP, who was very good. I made an appointment, what did I have to lose? I walked into the doctor's office in my gym gear and waited forty-five minutes past my appointment time to see him.

I sat in his office and immediately broke into tears. He took one look at me in my gym gear - we both knew I was not going to the gym; he asked me a few questions, smiled gently and told me he thought I was having a breakdown.

Relief flooded me, finally. There was something wrong with me, it had not all been in my imagination. I cried even harder as he organised with the mental health nurse to see me twice a week. He prescribed antidepressants as well, but I did not take them for long, they did not really help.

With the help of the nurse, I began to make progress, it was slow, but I was moving in the right direction. She explained that I had boxed myself in so much that there was no room left to breathe. I never told her about my recreational drug use because it did not occur to me that it could have been one of the reasons for the breakdown. We talked about my alcoholism and my recovery; she did not suggest I go to an Alcoholics Anonymous meeting to see if that would have helped me.

Mother's Day

My Darling Charlie,

I know those last few years at school were tough for you, they were for me too. I wanted so much to be the dynamic mother I had been in your early childhood. I did not want to be the mother I became.

At the time I saw myself as doing okay in difficult circumstances, but I was putting up a huge front. I smiled and laughed my way through it all, but really, I was dying inside. I was trying so hard to keep everything together, it was like being in a pressure cooker.

The one thing that helped keep me sane was going to work every day. Even in the darkest moments I continued to work hard because I knew I needed to keep a roof over our heads and to pay your school fees. Working with the elderly helped to keep everything in perspective; advice that was given over a cup of tea gave me a new way of looking at being a parent.

The house we were living in was torture, it drained my positive energy to the point where if I had stayed home all weekend, I would have slept the whole time. I reasoned that going out on the weekends was better for both of us. I was not avoiding you! Did you think I was neglecting you?

I was taking on extra work as you were stealing money out of my purse. Yes, I knew, and yes, I was disappointed in you, but then on some subconscious level I knew I was not managing my money properly.

When you found your first job, I was so proud of you. I hoped that you would learn that money can come and go very quickly, and that while I did not expect you to contribute to the household, I hoped you could understand why I made you responsible for paying for any extra things you wanted.

I was in a constant state of fight or flight for such a long time, I was relieved when I finally found a doctor who saw me as depressed. With his help and guidance, I began see my own inner light again and started to recognise the determined Wendy of old.

As the days moved closer to you finishing school, I felt like I had made some good decisions: moving into a nicer house within walking distance of your school, a house that I felt safe in again helped both of us. The heavy cloud that had been a heavy prescience began to lift and I finally felt like there was hope again.

While those last two years would be tumultuous, we both achieved a great deal, didn't we? I hope that life brings some sunshine, for both of us.

Love always.
Mum

Chapter 17

Four years after we had moved into the dark and dingy house I was at breaking point; I knew I could no longer stay there. With a teenager entering the last couple of years of high school, cutting down the travelling time would provide more time for the workload demands of the senior years. More importantly, although I was in a much better place mentally – thanks to the care I had received – I knew that, in order to continue my recovery, I needed to be in a more welcoming and supportive living environment.

As I searched for a place within walking distance of St Rita's, I realised the rents they were asking were way beyond my budget. To make this work, I would need to find someone to share. Margie, who worked in the office at the agency was also house hunting, we were of a similar age and had shared interests. After dozens of inspections, we finally found a house that ticked all our boxes and a few extras. I could even walk to work if I wanted to, which I did on occasion. We settled in and I felt a sense of stability once again.

As part of the arrangement we made, Margie agreed to watch over my now sixteen-year-old for two weeks while I took a much-needed break. This would be my first real holiday, not just a trip to Murray to see the family. I was planning a longer trip to Europe for myself once my child finished school and officially became an adult, so this was to be a taster. Both of my housemates seemed happy to see me go; I took the step and booked a trip to Bali with friends.

The trip was coordinated by Chloe; it was a package deal that provided for our flights plus four nights in Kuta. We would find our own accommodation for the rest of our stay.

I had no idea what to expect, I had only had glimpses of Bali through travel shows. I expected it to be hot, but the heatwave that hit us when we got off the plane was like after walking into a wall of fire.

The next shock came when we took a taxi to the hotel. It was worse than any peak hour traffic I had ever experienced. What seemed like thousands of scooters were zipping in and out of lanes with multiple people on them, sometimes whole families.

Our hotel had a decent sized pool, and it was lovely to get into the cool refreshing water. We stayed at the hotel for an hour or so, before going out to explore. Chloe and CC had been to Bali before and went over a few things, including warning me of the bartering I would be expected to engage in. I have never been good at haggling and my lack of skill was about to be proven.

Shopping was high on my to-do list. I wanted to get all my Christmas gifts, as everything is ridiculously cheap there. It was first chance in my life that I would have to buy decent presents for my ever-expanding family.

We waited until late afternoon before heading to the Poppies Lane markets. In Bali there is a superstition around being the first to attend a stall on any given day – you are obligated to buy something, or the stall holders believe they will have bad luck all day. We were standing in front of a row of colourful stalls when CC said sternly, "Wendy, you have to barter, barter, barter!"

I joked that I would not be "buying, buying, buying", only "looking, looking, looking", but she had me worried and I made them promise not to leave my side. As we wandered up and down the streets I managed to get ahead of the others, but I was not too worried as I was sure they were not too far away.

I stopped in front of a stall selling luxury brand purses, backpacks and handbags. To my eye they looked like the real thing: Chanel, Prada, you name it they had it. There were two sisters, four sisters-in-law and my two sisters plus Mum and Penny to buy for, and there was also a great Nike bag a teenager would love that could be used for school sports or travel. My resolve to 'just look' was forgotten in my excitement.

Exciting about getting all my shopping done in one go, I selected nine items and asked for the prices. Not being familiar with the exchange rate, and with limited Rupiahs in my bag I was calculating the amount I would need in Aussie Dollars when I looked up and found myself being circled by the shopkeeper's wife and family. I suddenly felt trapped, hoping my friends would show up soon. I tried to barter, but the stallholder was insistent, he would not come down to the price I suggested. My face dropped as I realised the amount they were asking was more than the money I had on me.

I really wanted all the things I had selected. I gave in when they offered to take me to the ATM to get the rest of the money. Chloe and CC looked surprised to see me going past on the back of a scooter, shouting that I would be back soon.

I was so pleased with the bargain I had scored, only to be laughed at by my friends who knew I could have got a much better deal. Secretly I still think I did okay, paying the equivalent of seventy-five Australian Dollars for nine purses and the sports bag. I would never have got such a great price at home.

Chloe and CC stayed closer to me after that.

I was like a whirlwind passing through the streets of Bali for the first two days, wanting to see and do everything. I felt that if I did not do it now, the chance would be gone forever. The girls pointed out to me that we were on holiday, and something in those words made sense in my brain and I slowed down, took a breath and relaxed.

I had never in my life experienced going slow, I was forever on the go, never stopping to really appreciate what was going on around me. Even on Bali time, we hardly stopped for the first five days, doing tours into the countryside and up into the mountains, drinking 'civet coffee' that was actually made from the animals' poop, buying genuine silver jewellery in small towns, and dining in traditional Balinese restaurants that only the locals knew about. We paid around five Australian Dollars for a three-course meal and drinks.

We drank cocktails – or in my case, mocktails – in swanky resorts overlooking the ocean, visited temples and rode horses along the beaches. We lay on the beach soaking up the sun, bought trinkets and sarongs and had massages by a ninety-year-old woman with the strength of a twenty-year-old.

At one of the hotels, I logged into the computer and Facetimed home, only to be told that I was on holiday and should be focusing on having a good time. While it was reassuring that things were going well back in Australia, I felt a little sad that I had not been missed.

The rest of our trip was spent in Legian relaxing by the pool or on the beach. CC and Chloe drank Bintangs, I drank Coke. By the end of the trip, we all had great tans. I read a novel for the first time in ages. I loved the peace and serenity of the countryside.

When it was time to come home, I was not ready. I was so relaxed that I had to be dragged onto the plane.

We arrived home in the early hours of the morning it was lightly raining. I woke a few hours later suffering from Bali Belly, it took a couple of days to get over it. Margie gave me slippery elm tablets, which helped to manage the worst of the symptoms. My teenager was happy with the bag and the other trinkets I had brought back, but was more excited about a holiday trip up north with Jessie's sisters later in the year, to be taken without me. Year Eleven was not even finished and our lives were already heading in different directions.

The rain that was falling the day I arrived home from Bali did not stop for the rest of the year, and my holiday memories were soon forgotten as I got back into the demands of my work and parenting roles.

❖

It had been a funny year, a mix of highlights and sorrows. There were a few deaths of those close to me, including a client named Hugh. I had become close to him and his wife

Lanie, I even left my community care role to become his full-time carer until he passed away.

Watching Hugh dying in front of me was a harrowing experience, it shook me to my core. I began to smoke again. I stayed with him in the hospital the night before he died; he was due to have an operation the following day and he asked me if I thought he would get through it. I said, "Of course you will, do not worry you will see me again.".

I went home in the morning so that I could have a sleep, but before I had settled down, Hugh's daughter called and said I needed to come back to the hospital as they did not think he was going to make it. I rushed to the hospital and parked my car across the road at the shopping centre as I could not afford the parking fee. I rushed up to Hugh's room. "See, I said you would see me again!". He passed away early the next morning, I was there by his side with Lanie and his daughters.

When I got back to my car, I found it had been broken into. Nothing was stolen, but everything, including my personal items had been thrown out of my car and spread across the carpark. I burst into tears of combined rage and sorrow.

Mortality was everywhere. Two women that I knew from the coast had been diagnosed with cancer, one was only twenty-eight the other in her mid-thirties. Both died within months of each other.

Even closer to home, my beautiful mother Sally had a heart attack. She was only fifty years old. Nathan called me early one morning to let me know she was okay but was in hospital under observation. She had been under a lot of stress, having married a man who was unfaithful and who caused her a lot of financial stress. Mum would have to sell our family home to free herself of the debt.

The rest of the year passed quickly, and soon it was time to travel home to Murray for our family Christmas and New Year. Tommy was to have his twenty first birthday in the new year as well. After all that had happened, it was nice to go home. It was also nice to be away from the rain in Brisbane.

As we travelled home from Murray in the New Year we followed our usual ritual and stopped at Sarah's in Cotton on the way. After she greeted us, Sarah asked if I had been listening to the radio news.

I knew the rain had been constant, but I had no idea that while we had been driving Southern Queensland was in flood. The border was to be closed at five pm that day, there was no way I was going to make it in time. I called Mandy to tell her my return to work would be delayed, I would not be starting work as planned on Wednesday, that Karinga would be in flood. She laughed and said she did not think so.

On Wednesday morning I watched the TV news in horror. Water was gushing through the streets of Karinga. I felt so helpless, I fretted for my brother Sam and his wife who were living in one of the areas affected by the rising flood waters. When I finally got hold of him, the worst had passed and their house was saved, as was ours, being on top of a hill.

I did not want to put my child at risk of being in or near flood waters, so we waited in Cotton for four more days before I felt it was safe to travel home. As we drove along the highway towards Karinga late that night I was struck by the eeriness as we passed through the suburbs. Everything was in darkness; the smell of rotten food and raw sewage was terrible. I was forced to take several detours to get to our house as flood water still covered the roads. So many houses were lost, the building where I worked was destroyed, along with the work vehicles. Two of the carers who were on the road during the floods lost their own cars. One of my friends lost her house, thankfully no one was killed or injured.

The rain stopped as we arrived home, but as the sun came out the stench continued for a few weeks while people mopped up, demolished, or walked away from their homes.

❖

Slowly the city rebuilt itself and life went back to normal. With a seventeen-year-old now in the last year of school. I was proud of the efforts we had both made to get this far in life.

Margie had met a nice man named Bert; he stayed with us whenever he was home from the mines. We all got along, though about halfway through the year Margie started being angry at silly little things. Tension was rising; it was not something I wanted my Year 12 student to be living with. We stayed away as much as possible, hiding in our bedrooms or staying out to avoid Margie and her temper. It was unfortunate that neither of us could afford the rent on our own, it was almost half my fortnight earnings.

The problems escalated as the year progressed. By the time the Year 12 formal came around. I had agreed to a small after party at our house. Margie was unhappy about this and said she was worried the kids would steal her things. She put a lock on her door and went out for the night.

Jessie had been invited to attend the party. He drove up to Karinga with a friend. My brother Sam, who was working as an apprentice mechanic, borrowed a nice car to drive the kids to the formal.

The day arrived, and our house swelled with kids getting ready. Grace, Ruby, and their husbands came over to help with supervision. Jessie was nowhere to be found, and despite dozens of calls and texts asking when he would be arriving, he stopped answering his phone. My anxiety was growing.

Sam's wife and I did not really get along very well. She was very clingy and controlling of Sam's time. She also liked to hog the limelight. It irritated me as although we were a very close family, she seemed to have convinced Sam that we did not really love him like her family did.

As the night of the formal approached, my anxiety and impatience were growing by the minute. My effort to make everything perfect for my only child was made all the more difficult due to the Jessie's betrayal, which I was trying my best to keep hidden, and also due to the growing disdain I was experiencing from my sister-in-law. I managed to keep it together until Sam had set of, chauffeuring the kids to the formal. It was a real treat to see my brother sitting in the driver's seat and the kids in the back, he was the real deal.

Meanwhile, my sister-in-law was sulking in a corner because I had not relented and allowed her to sit in the front alongside Sam. This was the kids' night, not hers. After they were happily on their way, I was able to finally let my guard down and vent my frustrations to my friends.

I was also angry at Jessie for being such a bastard to our child. I could not comprehend why he would be so mean, but I now understand it was because, just like my sister-in-law, he did not like that it was not all about him, that he was not the star of the show. He was simply chucking an adult tantrum, to the detriment of his child's happiness. When I was asked about Jessie's whereabouts, I had no option but to say I had not heard from him, which was the truth.

Margie had been worried about complaints from the neighbours, so I registered the party at the local police station. The police officer had asked if there would be underage drinking, I responded that I would not be supplying alcohol, but I could not guarantee that other parents would be that thoughtful. He was taken back by my honesty. I had left notes in the neighbour's letter boxes outlining that there was to be a party, that it had been registered with the police and that it would be shut down by two am.

As the kids arrived home, they were given arm bands. We told them they were to only use plastic cups and informed them they would be leaving by two am. I shut up the front of the house, turned off the lights and locked the door. I saw a patrol car go past and waved.

I thought the kids would put up a fight at the end of the night, but when I said, "OK kids, it's time to start cleaning up and organising your way home.", they all moved into action. At two am my backyard was clean and tidy and all the kids who were not staying had gone.

After the party, my insightful teenager told me that they did not have to be mad at their father, because I was mad enough for both of us. Hearing those beautiful words, I felt a sense of release and burst into tears. Yet even with that kind of level-headed acceptance from someone so young, I still felt devastated by the total disregard towards our child on this special occasion.

Mother's Day

The stress of the weekend showed in my body, my neck and shoulders had seized badly so I went to see Dr Bruce the next day. He banned me from driving until the middle of the week, and because he had been treating my mental health he was happy to give me extra sick days to cover my time off. I felt mentally incapable of going back to work and handling the questions of my workmates and clients about the weekend. They had all been so excited about the formal and knew the effort I had made to ensure its success, I just couldn't face telling them the truth about the issues with Sam's wife and about Jessie's non-appearance.

In addition to my weakened emotional state, my friendship with Margie was by now finally unravelling. The mood in the house was like one of slow death. I walked on eggshells to avoid upsetting her further and to try and keep the house peaceful for the approaching end of year exams. I offered to move out, even finding another rental within my price range and only a little further from the school. Margie went into a fit of rage and told me that even if I moved out, I would have to continue paying rent on our house as well. I felt like I was being crushed under a rock.

❖

The one positive in this situation was that Beau was back in my life. We had reconnected at Sally's fiftieth birthday; he was newly single and it was nice to finally have him as my friend again. I was conscious of the conversation I had with Grant all those years ago, and I still felt a responsibility to honour that promise I made him.

Beau was still living near Eureka when I got up the courage to tell him how I felt. My heart raced as I placed the call, not knowing if he still felt the same about me. What would I do if he rejected me?

I decided it was worth the risk to try, otherwise I would always wonder. I had been through so much in my life and I was beginning to realise I had to take a chance. I did not want to die with regrets.

I told Beau how I felt about him. At first, there was silence at the end of the phone. I began to apologise, but he cut me off, saying he felt the same, that he had always loved me. My heart lifted. I stood up, bent forward and straightened up again as my body released itself from the grip I had it in.

We arranged that Beau would come to Karinga for my birthday. I was so excited.

The tension in the house got to a boiling point when we received our electricity bill. It was astronomical. Margie blamed me for using an oil heater, though I knew Bert had kept a fan heater going in their bedroom for up to eight hours a day. I gave Margie the ultimatum to either pay half the bill, or to move out and I would keep her share of the bond. To my relief, she decided to move out. She knew I would have to pay the rent on my own for the remaining couple of months and thought I would not be able to cope.

Despite the strain of the past year, or perhaps because it seemed like the problems were all coming to an end, my thirty-seventh birthday was one of the best days of my life. Margie moved out and Beau arrived. Year 12 was almost over, and I was making early plans for my trip to Europe. For the first time in years, I was looking forward to the future, and what life had in store.

THE END – *NOT QUITE!*

Coming Soon

Book 2:

One Day at a Time

Still reeling from the shock of her only child's baffling rejection, Wendy packs her bags and heads to Europe for the trip of a lifetime, quite unaware that she has brought along some extra baggage as well. While discovering a whole new world, Wendy finds that her past will not let her go and will shortly rocket her into an unexpected future.

Find out how Wendy battles her demons and whether she wins the war in the next phase of her life.

Available November 2021.

CPSIA information can be obtained
at www.ICGtesting.com
Printed in the USA
BVHW031332260423
663002BV00007B/481

9 780645 114508